John George Hodgins

**Easy Lessons in General Geography**

with maps and illustrations

John George Hodgins

**Easy Lessons in General Geography**
*with maps and illustrations*

ISBN/EAN: 9783337391201

Printed in Europe, USA, Canada, Australia, Japan

Cover: Foto ©Andreas Hilbeck / pixelio.de

More available books at **www.hansebooks.com**

LOVELL'S SERIES OF SCHOOL-BOOKS.

# EASY LESSONS

IN

# GENERAL GEOGRAPHY,

## WITH MAPS AND ILLUSTRATIONS;

BEING INTRODUCTORY TO "LOVELL'S GENERAL GEOGRAPHY."

BY J. GEORGE HODGINS, LL.B., F.R.G.S.,

AUTHOR OF "GEOGRAPHY AND HISTORY OF THE BRITISH COLONIES, "LOVELL'S GENERAL GEOGRAPHY," ETC.

"The study of Geography is both profitable and delightful."—*Milton.*

𝔐𝔬𝔫𝔱𝔯𝔢𝔞𝔩:
PRINTED AND PUBLISHED BY JOHN LOVELL, ST. NICHOLAS STREET;
AND FOR SALE AT THE BOOKSTORES.
1872.

# PREFACE.

LOVELL'S "GENERAL GEOGRAPHY" having already had such an extensive sale as to establish it in the favour of the educational public, it might be said that another work on the same subject was unnecessary; but the "GENERAL GEOGRAPHY" being considered by intelligent teachers as too far advanced for young beginners, the Author, at the request of Mr. LOVELL, the enterprising publisher of a valuable series of School-Books for Canada, has consented to prepare, for use in junior classes, the following "EASY LESSONS IN GENERAL GEOGRAPHY.

The EASY LESSONS are intended to be merely introductory to the larger work; and they are designed as far as possible, simply to form a brief outline of that work. The Author has, however, adopted a slightly different plan (original so far as he has been able to learn) in the preparation of this book. He has, in the first place, sought to embody, in easy and familiar language, a Conversational Sketch of each division of the subject to which the attention of the pupil is directed. He has then inserted a series of questions on the principal points of that sketch; and has supplied, where deemed necessary, appropriate answers to those questions.

These Conversational Sketches are also intended to promote another important object; namely, the providing of easy Geographical Reading-Lessons for junior classes, which description of lessons is not to be found in the authorized National Readers.

The "*Conversational Trip*" through each of the principal countries in the world, is designed to connect, in the mind of the pupil, the objects and associations of travel with a geographical knowledge of the more important physical features of coast-line, mountain, river, &c. The Review-Lessons, in connection with these Conversational Trips, will tend to fix the knowledge thus acquired, still deeper in the mind of the learner.

As already intimated, the general arrangement of these "EASY LESSONS" is similar to that of the larger work; and many of the definitions in the introductory part are the same. This will render the study of the "GENERAL GEOGRAPHY" itself more easy and agreeable to the pupil, while the disadvantage of using an entirely new larger book will be avoided. The one gives a rapid and general view of the subject, suited to a beginner; the other is more minute and thorough, as well as better adapted to the more advanced pupil.

Although the Author has no pecuniary interest in either the "EASY LESSONS" or the "GENERAL GEOGRAPHY," he cannot but express his grateful thanks to those influential persons who have so kindly expressed to the publisher their high opinion of the Author's humble labours in the preparation of the latter work. He is more than gratified, also, at the success which has attended the publication and sale of the "GENERAL GEOGRAPHY;" and for this reason he submits the present little work, with the anticipation and hope that it will meet with at least a portion of that favour which has been shown to his larger Geography.

J. G. H.

TORONTO, 3rd October, 1862.

# EASY LESSONS IN GENERAL GEOGRAPHY.

"HE....HANGETH THE EARTH UPON NOTHING."—Job xxvi. 7.

Fig. 1.—THE SUN, EARTH, MOON, STARS, AND CLOUDS, IN THE HEAVENS.

## PART I.

[Before beginning our regular lessons, we shall explain a few things which boys and girls see every day, but which they do not understand. We hope that they will pay attention to what we say, and try to remember it.]

### CONVERSATION OR READING LESSON No. I.

#### Introductory Sketch.

1. When boys and girls awake in the morning, that which helps them to see the things around them is the beautiful light of day.

2. At first they do not know where the light comes from; but if they get up very early on a clear morning, they will see that it comes from the bright round Sun, which appears to be slowly rising out of the ground, or trees, or water.

3. As they watch the Sun, they see that it rises higher in the sky (as in Fig. 1), and gets brighter; so that in a short time they cannot look at it, for it dazzles their eyes too much.

4. The Sun always appears to rise in the east, and to set in the west. At noon it is high up in the southern sky, and then the shadows of houses, trees, &c., point toward the north. In the morning the shadows point toward the west, and in the evening toward the east.

5. After 12 o'clock in the day, the Sun appears to come down lower and lower in the sky; so that toward evening it seems to be very near the ground again.

6. By and by it goes quite out of sight; and then (if the night is fine) the Stars, and perhaps the Moon, appear in the sky.

7. The Stars are of different sizes: some twinkle very brightly, while others can scarcely be seen.

8. The new Moon, when first seen, looks like a silver bow. Every night it rises later than on the previous one; and for a fortnight it grows larger and rounder, until it is "at the full." After this it begins to get smaller

again; until at last it disappears, and cannot be seen again until the next month.

9. The Moon has no light of its own: it gets all its light from the Sun. It has always the same shape, and is nearly round. As however it is quite dark itself, we can at first only see as it were a narrow strip of the silvery bow: this is that part of it upon which the Sun shines.

10. Each night we see a little more of this silvery part; until at last the Moon is "at the full," and then we see what is called a "Full Moon."

11. Although the Sun and the Moon appear to be about the same size in the sky, they are not so in reality. The Moon is only the one forty-ninth part of the size of our Earth; while the Sun (which is so very far off that it does not look very large) is 500 times greater than the Earth, the Moon, and all the Stars which revolve around it put together.

12. The Moon looks much larger than any of the Stars, because it is much nearer to us; but many of the Stars are hundreds of times larger than the Moon. Boys know how large a kite or a balloon looks when it is on the ground, and how small it looks when high up in the air: it is just so with the size and appearance of the Sun, Moon, and Stars.

13. Now it will seem strange to our little reader to hear that the Sun does not rise at all (though it appears to do so); but that it is the turning round of the Earth which makes the Sun appear to rise. For as the Earth (which is like a great ball) is constantly spinning round like a top, each part of it turns toward the Sun as it moves. Thus that part of the Earth on which a boy or girl lives, begins every morning to approach the Sun. At noon we are as near the Sun as we can be during the day. We then begin to turn from it, and at midnight we are as far away as we can be during the night. Other places on the Earth, in their turn, get near and far from it also.

14. It will surprise little boys and girls to know that not only the Sun and the Earth, but the Moon and the Stars also, never leave the sky at all, though they are all constantly changing their positions there. During the daytime the light of the Sun is so much

brighter than the light of the Stars, that we cannot see their little twinkle. Many of the Stars are a great deal larger than this whole Earth; but as they are so very far off, they appear like mere specks, and we can only just see them. Others, from their being nearer to us, are brighter than the rest.

15. The Earth turns round once in about 24 hours. An imaginary line through the centre of the Earth (on which the Earth turns) is called its axis. The ends of this axis are called poles. Turning 12 hours toward the Sun makes it light; turning 12 hours from the Sun makes it dark. But as the north and south ends (or poles) of the Earth turn very slowly to or from the Sun, months (instead of hours, as with us) of light, twilight, darkness, and then twilight, light, &c., again, succeed each other there continually. As we come away from the north and south poles, the days and nights become more of an equal length. When the days are long, the nights are short; and when the nights are long, the days are short. While we have day, other places have night; and while we have night, other places have day.

---

## EXAMINATION OR REVIEW LESSON No. I.

### The Earth and its Appearance.

*Q.* Where does the light of day come from?

*A.* From the Sun, which appears to rise up in the sky every morning.

*Q.* In what direction does the Sun appear to travel in the sky?

*A.* From east to west, along the southern sky.

*Q.* When the Sun is out of sight at night, what do we see if the sky is clear?

*A.* The Stars; and also the Moon at her regular times of appearing.

*Q.* Does the Sun rise every morning, as he appears to do?

*A.* No: it is the Earth which turns round and brings him into view every morning.

*Q.* Where are the Stars during the day?

*A.* In the sky; but as the Sun shines so brightly, they cannot be seen.

*Q.* Whence do the Moon and Stars get their light?

*A.* The Moon gets her light from the Sun;

hich are very far off,
ind are supposed to be

 the Moon?
are in reality much
 but they all appear
much farther off.
e Earth to turn round once?
iving us on an average
nd 12 hours of night.

___

TION II.

d its Divisions.

rls know what is the
*ight.* A day and a
ek, a week forms part
forms part of a year.
n the first day of Jan-
: rather 365¼, days in
r the quarter-day, one
he February of every
s called "leap-year."
ded into 12 months,
 on an average.
re divided into what
 Thus March, April,
*pring ;* June, July,
September, October,
 or "the Fall,"—for
s fall; and December,
*Winter.*
 Spring; for during
 the flowers *spring* up
bud on the trees and
 birds come from the
ir nests and to sing
 farmer, too, is busy
l planting.
 not too hot, is very
n are the longest of
 girls can play and
hearts' content. The
l beautiful, and all

with it the rich reward
. Fruit, grain, and
athered in rich abun-
 God's goodness in

bountifully supplying our daily wants. The Autumn also reminds us of the close of life ; for then the leaves wither and fall from the trees, and the birds take their flight to lands where summer is just commencing.

7. Winter comes; and with it frost, snow, and storms. We then seek warmth and protection from the cold ; and cattle seek shelter. This is the time for skating (and sleigh-riding. The long winter evenings, too, bring with them time to prepare for school, as well as to enjoy the reading of pleasant books from the school or the home library ; for good boys and girls read and study, as well as play.

8. The regularity with which these Seasons come round, should remind us of God's faithful promise to Noah (of which the beautiful rainbow is the token), that he would never again destroy the World and its inhabitants with water; but that "while the earth remaineth, seedtime and harvest, and cold and heat, and summer and winter, and day and night, shall not cease."—Genesis viii. 22.

___

## EXAMINATION LESSON II.

### Time and its Divisions.

*Q.* Name the principal divisions of time.

*A.* Seconds, minutes, hours, days, weeks, months, and years.

*Q.* Can you repeat the time-table?

*A.* Yes: 60 seconds make 1 minute.
60 minutes " 1 hour.
24 hours " 1 day.
7 days " 1 week.
4 weeks " 1 lunar* month.
13 lunar months, or } make 1 civil year.
12 calendar months, }

*Q.* How many days and weeks are in a year?

*A.* 365¼ days, or 52 weeks.

*Q.* How many days are there in each month?

*A.* Thirty days hath September,
April, June, and November:
February hath twenty-eight alone,
And all the rest have thirty-one;
But leap-year coming once in four,
February then hath one day more.

*Q.* Into how many seasons is the year divided?

*A.* Into four, called Spring, Summer, Autumn, and Winter.

* From the Latin word *Luna,* the Moon.

*Q. Name the months in each season.*

*A.* The *Spring* months are March, April, and May; *Summer*, June, July, and August; *Autumn*, September, October, and November; *Winter*, December, January, and February.

*Q. Describe, in your own words, the seasons of Spring, Summer, Autumn, and Winter.*

*Q. What promise did God make to Noah in regard to the certainty of the return of these seasons?*

## CONVERSATION III.

### Sketch of Geography.

1. The word Ge-og-rä-phy (which is derived from two Greek words) means a "writing about the Earth." We now understand Geography to be a description of the Earth, of its people, and of its products.

2. If the Earth were an immense flat surface (which it looks like, and which people in the olden times used to think it was), we could see a great deal more of it at one time than we do; and with a telescope we could see more still. But the Earth is an immense round ball shaped something like an orange.

3. This can be proved if we stand on the shore of a lake or of the sea and look at a ship coming toward us. At first we can just see the top of its masts, then the hull or body of the ship, and afterward the full size of the ship. This varying appearance which a ship or any other moving object has from the shore, is the same all round the Globe. (See Fig. 2.)

4. For convenience, Geography has been divided into three parts. The first part is called *Math-e-mat-i-cal* or *As-tro-nom-i-cal Geography*, because it relates to the connection of the Earth with the Sun, Moon, and Stars; the second part is called *Phys-i-cal Geography*, because it relates to the land and water divisions of the Earth's surface; and the third part is called *Po-lit-i-cal Geography*, because it relates to the various nations on the Earth, and to the boundaries of different countries.

## EXAMINATION LESSON III.

### What Geography Teaches.

*Q. What is this book intended to teach you?*

*A.* General Geography.

*Q. What is General Geography?*

*A.* A general description of the Earth.

*Q. What is the Earth?*

*A.* The great Globe on which we live.

*Q. Who made the Earth?*

*A.* "In the beginning God created the heaven and the earth."—Genesis i. 1.

*Q. What appearance does the Earth present to us?*

*A.* It appears to us to be nearly flat, and to be covered overhead with a lofty sky, which seems to over-arch us like a dome.

*Q. Is this a correct description of the Earth?*

*A.* No: the Earth is rounded like an orange, as shown in Figures 1 and 2; and has the sky on all sides of it, as shown in Fig. 1.

Fig. 2.—ROTUNDITY OF THE EARTH ILLUSTRATED.

*Q. How can we prove that the Earth is round?*

*A.* By the appearance of a ship at sea. At first we can only see the top of its masts; but afterward, as it comes nearer, its full size.

*Q. Into how many branches is Geography usually divided, and name them?*

*A.* Three,—Math-e-mat-i-cal or As-tro-nom-i-cal, Phys-i-cal, and Po-lit-i-cal Geography.

*Q. What is Mathematical or Astronomical Geography?*

*A.* A description of the Sun, Moon, and Stars; and of the Earth, as one of the planets in the Heavens.

*Q. What is Physical Geography?*

*A.* A description of the natural divisions of land and water on the Globe.

*Q. What is meant by the Natural Divisions of the Earth?*

*A.* The divisions formed by nature, such as Islands, Lakes, Seas, Oceans, &c.

*Q.* What is Political Geography?

*A.* A description of the various political divisions of the World, and of the extent of different countries.

*Q.* What is meant by the Political Divisions of the World?

*A.* Those divisions of the World which have been formed by man; such as King-doms, Empires, and Re-pub-lics.

---

## CONVERSATION IV.

### Something about the Hemispheres.

1. The Earth is also called a *Planet*, a *World*, a *Ball*, a *Globe*, and a *Sphere*. It is called a *planet* because it moves through the Heavens; it is called a *world* because it is an inhabited part of God's great Creation ; and it is called a *ball, globe*, or *sphere* because it is rounded in shape.

2. As the Earth is shaped like a ball, we have to picture it either on a globe, or by a drawing called a map. As we turn round a globe, we can see each side of it; but on a map we have to picture each side separately.

3. As we cannot make a drawing or picture large enough to show every river, mountain, sea, ocean, or city on the Earth in its full size, we have to represent them on a map. But as the Earth is round, we can only show, on a drawing, half of it at one view. Such a drawing is called a hem-I-sphere, or half a sphere. On this drawing we put a number of round or curved lines to show that the Earth is round, and to point out where each place on its surface is situated. (See Fig. 3.)

4. These hemispheres have various names. The two usually shown on a map are called the Eastern and Western Hemispheres. These hemispheres show all the world east and west of Europe, where Geography was first taught. The Northern and Southern Hemispheres show those parts of the Earth north or south of the Equator,—of which we shall hear by and by. If you look on the map, or on the following figure, you will see all the land and water divisions in each hemisphere.

## EXAMINATION LESSON IV.

### The Hemispheres.

*Q.* What is the Earth called?

*A.* A Planet, a World, a Ball, a Globe, or a Sphere.

*Q.* How is the World pictured to us?

*A.* Either on a globe or by a map.

*Q.* Which is the most natural way of showing us the whole Earth?

*A.* On a globe ; for we can then see its different sides, and how the land and water are connected.

*Q.* How is the Earth, when it is shown on a map, made to look like a ball?

*A.* By means of the curved or circular lines which are drawn upon it to make it appear round, as on Fig. 3.

*Q.* How is it that we can only see one-half of the round World on a map?

*A.* Because as the paper is flat, so the surface of the map is flat also, which makes it impossible to show on it in one picture more than half of a round body.

*Q.* How, then, is the other half of the whole World shown?

*A.* By means of a second map, which shows the other half.

*Q.* What are these halves called?

*A.* Hemispheres, or half-globes.

*Q.* Which two are most generally shown or used in Geographies?

*A.* The Eastern and Western Hemispheres.

*Q.* Why are they called the Eastern and Western Hemispheres?

*A.* Because the chief part of the land and water described in them lies to the east and to the west of Europe, where Geography was first taught.

WESTERN HEMISPHERE.

Engr. for Easy Lessons in Gen'l Geography

EASY LESSONS IN GENERAL GEOGRAPHY.

*Q.* Name and point out on the map the principal countries in this hemisphere.

*Q.* Name and point out the great oceans on the map.

*Q.* Name and point out, also, the position of the principal sea named.

*Q.* Name and point out the positions of the principal bays and gulfs.

*Q.* Name and point out the larger islands and island-groups on the map.

*Q.* Name and point out the principal capes.

*Q.* Name and point out the principal straits.

*Q.* Name and point out the different zones and tropics

*Q.* Name and point out the equator, the two poles, and the two circles.

*Q.* Name and point out the great mountain-ranges on the map.

*Q.* Name and point out the principal rivers.

EASTERN HEMISPHERE.

Engraved for Easy Lessons in Genl Geography.

Q. Name and point out on the map the continents and principal countries in this hemisphere.

Q. Name and point out the great oceans on the map.

Q. Name and point out, also, the positions of the principal seas.

Q. Name and point out the positions of the principal bays and gulfs.

Q. Name and point out the principal islands.

Q. Name and point out the principal capes.

Q. Name and point out the different zones and tropics

Q. Name and point out the equator, the two poles, and the two circles.

Q. Name and point out the great mountain-ranges on the map.

Q. Name and point out the principal rivers.

Q. Name and point out the principal straits or channel.

*Q.* Why is one of these divisions called also the Old World?

*A.* Because the Old World was first known to our forefathers, and in it man was created.

*Q.* Why is the other division called the New World?

*A.* Because the New World, discovered (it is said) by the Northmen about 800 years since, was re-discovered by Christopher Columbus and his companions only about 400 years ago.

*Q.* How do the proportions of land and water on the Eastern and Western Hemispheres compare?

*A.* The Eastern Hemisphere, or Old World, contains more land and less water than the Western Hemisphere.

*Q.* Name, and point out on the map, the great land-divisions in the Eastern Hemisphere.

*A.* Europe, Asia, Africa, and the island-continent of Aus-trā-lī-ă, which is part of O-ce-an-Ĭ-ă [o-she-].

*Q.* What are these great land-divisions called?

*A.* Con-tǐ-nents; except Oceania, which consists of great numbers of islands scattered over the ocean.

*Q.* What are the proportions of land and water on the Western Hemisphere?

*A.* The Western Hemisphere, or New World, contains a great deal more water than land.

*Q.* Name and point out the great land-divisions in the Western Hemisphere.

*A.* North and South America.

*Q.* Name and point out the two great clusters of islands in this Hemisphere.

*A.* The West-India Islands and the islands of Oceania.

*Q.* Into what other hemispheres can the World be divided?

*A.* Into the North Polar or Northern, and the South Polar or Southern, Hemispheres.

*Q.* Describe the North Polar or Northern Hemisphere.

*A.* The Northern Hemisphere includes all those regions lying between the North Pole and the Equator. It contains the principal land-divisions of the Globe.

*Q.* What circle and tropic are wholly in this hemisphere?

*A.* The Arc-tic Circle and the Tropic of Cancer.

*Q.* Describe the South Polar or Southern Hemisphere.

*A.* The Southern Hemisphere includes all those regions lying between the South Pole and

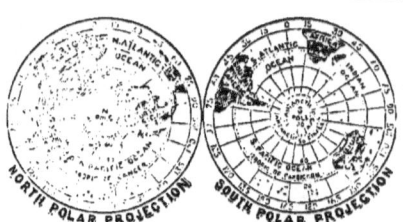

Fig. 4.—NORTHERN AND SOUTHERN HEMISPHERES, OR NORTH AND SOUTH POLAR PROJECTIONS.

the Equator. It contains the chief water-divisions of the Globe.

*Q.* What circle and tropic are wholly in this hemisphere.

*A.* The Ant-arc-tic Circle and the Tropic of Capricorn.

*Q.* What is the peculiarity of climate in the Southern Hemisphere?

*A.* In the Southern Hemisphere it is mid-summer in January, and mid-winter in June.

*Q.* Into what other Hemispheres is the World sometimes divided?

*A.* Into the Land and Water Hemispheres.

*Q.* Describe the Land-Hemisphere.

*A.* The Land-Hemisphere has Western Europe for its centre. It contains nearly all the land on the Earth's surface.

Fig. 5.—LAND AND WATER HEMISPHERES.

*Q.* Point out and name from Fig. 5 the principal land-division in the Land-Hemisphere.

*Q.* Describe the Water-Hemisphere.

*A.* The Water-Hemisphere has for its centre an island south-east of Australia. It contains nearly all the larger oceans and islands on the surface of the Globe.

*Q.* Point out and name from Fig. 5 the principal oceans n the Water-Hemisphere.

## CONVERSATION V.

### Sketch of the Mariner's Compass.

1. At first when persons wished to go by sea from one place to another, they had to keep in sight of land; or by watching the Sun by day and the Moon or Stars by night, they could steer the ship correctly. When they could not see the land, the Sun, the Moon, or the Stars, their risk of being lost was generally very great.

2. This difficulty lasted a long time. At length, Marco Polo, a celebrated Venetian traveller, brought from China, in the year 1260, a curious instrument, afterward called a mariner's compass, which consisted of a piece of lodestone placed upon cork and allowed to float on water. In this position the lodestone would turn toward the north.

3. Since Marco Polo's time, the compass has been greatly improved. It now consists of a piece of steel suspended on a point or pivot. This steel, when once touched by pieces of lodestone or magnet, continues to vibrate or turn until it points toward the north, or North Mag-net-ic Pole, to which it is attracted by a strong but unseen influence called Mag-net-ism.

Fig. 6.—THE MARINER'S COMPASS.

## EXAMINATION LESSON V.

### The Mariner's Compass.

Q. What is the Mariner's Compass?

A. An instrument chiefly for use at sea by mariners or sailors.

Q. Describe it as it appears at present.

A. It consists of a small bar of magnetized steel, called a needle, to which is attached a circular engraved card (Fig. 6), the whole being balanced on a pivot so as to turn round freely.

Q. In what direction does it point?

A. To the North, as shown in the engraving.

Q. Of what use is the compass?

A. It enables sailors and travellers to find their way across water and land; for as it always points in one direction, the position of any other place can easily be distinguished or known.

Q. Name the four principal points of the compass.

A. North, South, East, and West.

Fig. 7.—POINTS OF THE COMPASS SHOWN ON A MAP.

Q. How are these points shown on a map?

A. The North is shown at the top, and the South at the bottom; the East at the right hand, and the West at the left hand.

Q. Name the other parts of the compass as shown in the engraving.

A. North-East, South-East, North-West, and South-West.

Q. Why are the East, West, North, and South called the cardinal or chief points of the compass?

A. Because in the East the Sun appears to rise; in the West he appears to set; and because one end of the needle of the compass points to the North, and the other to the South.

## CONVERSATION VI.

### Conversational Trip over Land and Water.

[We shall now try to explain many things in Geography which little boys and girls often see, but do not understand.]

1. We should remember that were it not that books of Geography have been written, containing descriptions of the Earth and what is on its surface, people would have to travel over it in order to see the great cities, oceans, rivers, and mountains which cover its vast surface. Now, as many little boys and girls do not travel very far from home, they should be glad to learn from Geographies all about the wonderful World on which they live.

2. We shall now suppose our little learner to be taking a short trip with us away from home. We shall go with him and help to explain the names of many things which we shall see on our way.

3. But before setting out, we shall ask if our little travelling companion has not often thought that all the rest of the Earth was very small compared with the size of that part of it about his own home; and also if he does not think that only the place where he lives is over-arched by the beautiful blue sky. This Geography is designed to show him his mistakes in these and in other matters.

4. Any little boy who lives in the country has no doubt often seen a river, a lake, an island, or a mountain: but does he not often wonder where the great cities are, with their noise and bustle; and the wide ocean, with its storms and waves, its ships and steamers? On the other hand, any little boy who lives in a city must often wonder where the country is, with its trees and fields and meadows, for the sky seems to shut them all out.

5. After leaving home, the first thing we may see is a stream of water running across the road, having a bridge over it. When such a stream is large, it is called a "River," and the banks on either side are often high. If they are low and the stream is small, the stream is called a "Riv-ŭ-let," or, in America, "Creek." In other parts of the World, "Creek" means an in et of he sea. When the stream descends

over broken rocks, it is called a "Torrent"; and when over low rough rocks or large stones, it is called a Rapid "; but if it suddenly falls from a great height, as in the Niagara River, it is called a "Fall" or "Cat-ă-ract."

6. If we follow this stream, we may soon see it flow into a large open space of water. If this open space of water is wide, and has land on every side, it is called a "Lake"; and

Fig. 8.—A LAKE.

the land at the edge of the lake is called the "Shore." When one river flows into another, the first river is called a "Trib-u-tă-ry." The outlet of a river is called its "Mouth." Sometimes the river flows directly into the sea or ocean, and then its mouth, if wide and the tide flows into it, is called an "Es-tu-ă-ry."

7. Going farther along the road, we begin to ascend a high piece of ground. This is called a "Hill." If this piece of ground is very

Fig. 9.—A VOLCANO.

high and rocky, it is called a "Mountain"; and its top, when pointed, is called a "Peak." If a mountain throws out fire and smoke, it is called a "Vol-cā-no."

8. A connected series of mountains stretching across a country is called a "Mountain range"; and the space lying between two or more mountains is called a "Valley." If the space is very wide, it is called a "Plain." An immense plain with grass on it and no trees, is called a "Prairie" [pray-rĭ]. If this plain is sandy and is without grass, it is called a "Des-ert"; and any fertile spot on it is called an "O'-ă-sis."

9. And now we come near to a city or large town. (See Fig. 10.) Away in the distance on

Fig. 10.—CITY, HARBOUR, ROADSTEAD, CAPE, ETC.

the water we see the masts of ships. These ships have come across the ocean, which stretches away from country to country.

10. Some of the ships are quite near to the city, in a space of water called a "Har-bour"; others are farther away, at anchor in a place called a "Roadstead," beyond a piece of land which runs out into the water. This piece of land (as in Figs. 10 & 11) is called a "Cape": beyond it is a high and rocky cape, which is called a "Prom-on-tŏ-ry" or "Headland."

11. Outside the harbour (in Fig. 10) we see a piece of land standing alone in the water, with trees on it. This is an "Is-land." Islands are of various sizes, and are found alone or in clusters in the ocean. If in clusters (as in Fig. 12), the sea is there called an "Arch-i-pel-ă-go" [ark-ĭ-]. If what appears to be an island (in the same figure) is joined to the main land or shore, it is called a "Pen-in-su-lă" (or "almost an island"), and the place that joins it to the shore is called an "Isth-mus" (or "Neck").

12. Between us and the peninsula (in Figs. 10 & 12) we see a sheet of water nearly surrounded by the land, and quite sheltered. This is called a "Bay." When such a bay is so very large that we cannot see its size, and lose sight of land in crossing it, it is called a "Gulf" (such as the ulfs of Mexico and St. Lawrence).

13. Sometimes between a large island and the main land, or between two portions of main land, (as in Figs. 10 & 13,) there is a passage somewhat like a river. Such a passage is called a "Strait." If the

Fig. 11.—CAPE, PROMONTORY, AND COAST.

Fig. 12.—ARCHIPELAGO, PENINSULA, ISTHMUS, AND BAY.

strait is very wide, it is called a "Channel"; but if it is so shallow that a ship's lead may easily touch or *sound* its bottom, it is called a "Sound."

14. When we get into the city (Fig. 10), we shall see a great many things to interest us. If we go down near the ships, we shall see men taking out of them many things which grow or are made in countries far away,—and those countries this book will hereafter describe.

15. We have now completed our little trip, and hope it has been a pleasant and instructive one. We shall now ask a few questions on what we have seen or have helped to explain.

Fig. 13.—STRAIT, CHANNEL, ETC.

WESTERN HEMISPHERE.

EASTERN HEMISPHERE.

Fig. 14.—GREAT LAND AND WATER DIVISIONS ON THE GLOBE.

## EXAMINATION LESSON VI.

—

### Great Land and Water Divisions.

Q. What covers the surface of the Globe?

A. Land and water.

Q. Is there more land than water on the Globe?

A. No: there is only about one fourth as much land on the surface of the Globe as there is water.

Q. How is the land on the surface of the Globe divided?

A. Into five great divisions.

Q. What are they called?

A. Four are called Con-ti-nents; the fifth, called O-ce-an-i-ă [o-she-], is made up of a great many islands lying in one of the oceans.

Q. Name these Continents, and point them out on Fig.14.

A. Europe, Asia, Africa, and America.

Q. What are the greatest water-divisions of the Globe called?

A. Oceans.

Q. Describe an Ocean.

A. An Ocean is a vast body of salt water; and in stormy weather it has large, high waves.

*Q.* Do you know anything about the Ocean Tides?

*A.* Yes. At regular hours, the waters of an ocean overflow the land along the shore, and then flow off again : this is called a Tide.

*Q.* What about Ocean Currents?

*A.* The Ocean has also regular currents, when its waters flow steadily in one direction.

*Q.* Name some of the principal Ocean Currents.

*A.* The Polar and Eq-ua-to-ri-al [ck-wä-] Currents, and the Mexican Gulf-Stream.

*Q.* Name the Oceans, and point them out on Fig. 14.

*A.* The Atlantic, Pacific, Indian and Southern, Arctic, and Antarctic.

*Q.* Where is the Atlantic Ocean?

*A.* Between America, Europe, and Africa.

*Q.* Where is the Pacific Ocean?

*A.* Between America and Asia.

*Q.* Where are the Indian and Southern Oceans?

*A.* South of Asia, Africa, and America.

*Q.* Where are the Arctic and Antarctic Oceans?

*A.* The Arctic Ocean is at the North Pole, and the Antarctic at the South Pole.

## EXAMINATION LESSON VII.
—
### Divisions of Land on the Globe.

*Q.* Name the chief natural divisions of land.

*A.* Continents, Islands, Pen-in-su-las, Isthmus-es, and Capes.

*Q.* What is a Continent?

*A.* A vast portion of land containing many countries.

Fig. 15.—AN ISLAND (NEWFOUNDLAND).

*Q.* What is an Island?

*A.* A large or small piece of land with water all round it.

*Q.* What is a Peninsula?

*A.* A piece of land with water nearly all round it.

*Q.* What is an Isthmus?

*A.* A narrow neck or piece of land joining together two larger pieces of land.

*Q.* What is a Cape?

*A.* A piece of land stretching out into an ocean, a sea, or a lake.

Fig. 16.—PENINSULA (NOVA SCOTIA) AND ISTHMUS.

*Q.* Has a Cape any other names?

*A.* Yes : it is also called a Point, Head, Headland, and Promontory (or high rocky cape).

*Q.* What is a Prairie?

*A.* A great wide piece or tract of country nearly level, and chiefly covered with grass.

*Q.* What is a Plain?

*A.* A wide piece or tract of level country.

*Q.* What is a Desert?

*A.* A large piece or tract of barren country.

*Q.* What is an Oasis?

*A.* A fertile spot in a desert.

*Q.* What is a Mountain?

*A.* A very high hill; and its top, when pointed, is called a peak.

*Q.* What is a Mountain-range?

*A.* A number of mountains connected together and stretching along or across a country.

*Q.* What is a Volcano?

*A.* A burning mountain.

*Q.* What is the mouth of a Volcano called?

*A.* The crater; from which issue fire, smoke, and lava or volcanic cinders.

Fig. 17.—PICTORIAL ILLUSTRATIONS OF VARIOUS GEOGRAPHICAL TERMS.

REVIEW LESSON ON THE FOREGOING ILLUSTRATION.

*Q.* Point out on the above illustration, and describe in your own words, the following land-divisions:—Island,—Peninsula,—Isthmus,—Cape,—Promontory,—Coast,—Beach,—Mountain-range,—Volcano,—Valley,—Desert. Also the following water-divisions:— Ocean,— Sea,—Archipelago,—Gulf,—Bay,—Inlet,—Creek,—Lake,—Strait,—Sound,—Roadstead,—Harbour,—Port,—Source of River,—River,—Stream,—Waterfall,—Rapids,—Delta of River,—Canal.

*Q.* Point out in the illustration, and describe in your own words, the following objects on land:—Village,—Town,—City,—Capital,—Forest,—Railway,—Telegraph,—Fort,—Lighthouse.

*Q.* What is a Valley?

*A.* That part of a country lying between mountains or hills.

*Q.* What is a Coast or Shore?

*A.* That part of the land lying along the margin of an ocean, a sea, or a lake.

*Q.* What is a Beach?

*A.* The level part of a coast or shore.

## EXAMINATION LESSON VIII.

### Divisions of Water on the Globe.

*Q.* How is the water on the surface of the Globe divided?

*A.* Into Oceans, Seas, Lakes, Rivers, &c.

*Q.* What is an Ocean?

*A.* A great extent of water separating continents.

*Q.* What is a Sea?

*A.* A large space of water lying between countries.

*Q.* What is an Archipelago? (See Figs. 12 and 17.)

*A.* Part of an ocean or of a sea containing a number of islands.

*Q.* What is a Gulf?

*A.* A very large body of water stretching into the land.

*Q.* What is a Bay or Inlet?

*A.* A smaller body of water stretching into the land.

*Q.* What is a Lake?

*A.* A large or small body of water with land all round it (as in Figs. 8 and 17).

*Q.* What is a Pond?

*A.* A very small body of water.

*Q.* What is a Strait?

*A.* A narrow passage of water connecting two larger bodies of water (as in Fig. 13).

*Q.* What is a Channel?

*A.* A wider passage of water than a strait.

*Q.* What is a Sound?

*A.* A shallow strait or channel.

*Q.* What is a Harbour?

*A.* A sheltered place for ships.

*Q.* What is a River?

*A.* A large stream of fresh water running in a channel through, or over, the land.

*Q.* What are small streams of water called?

*A.* Rivulets, Rills, or Brooks.

*Q.* What is a Spring?

*A.* Water springing up out of the ground.

*Q.* What is a Waterfall?

*A.* Water falling over a bank or over rocks.

*Q.* What is a Rapid?

*A.* Water rapidly descending over rough stones or rocks; generally at a shallow portion of a river.

*Q.* What is a Delta?

*A.* Islands formed at and by the mouths of a river.

*Q.* What are those rivers called which flow into other rivers?

*A.* Branch Streams, Tributaries, or Affluents.

*Q.* What is a Canal?

*A.* An artificial channel of water like a river, formed for the passage of boats.

*Q.* What is a Swamp, Morass, or Bog?

*A.* A low, wet piece or tract of country.

*Q.* What is an Estuary?

*A.* The wide mouth of a river into which the sea tide flows.

## EXAMINATION LESSON IX.

### Various Objects on Land.

*Q.* Explain the difference between a Village and a Town.

*A.* A Village is a small collection of inhabited houses in the country; a Town is a larger collection of inhabited houses.

*Q.* Describe a City.

*A.* A City is a large town enjoying certain privileges conferred upon it by law.

*Q.* Describe a Capital.

*A.* A Capital is the seat of government and legislation in a country.

*Q.* Describe a Forest.

*A.* A Forest is a large tract of country covered naturally with trees and brushwood.

*Q.* Describe a Railway or Railroad.

*A.* A Railway or Railroad is a level roadway on which are laid two long lines of iron rails, a few feet apart, for the passage over them of carriages, which are chiefly propelled by steam.

*Q.* Describe an Electric Telegraph.

*A.* An Electric Telegraph is an invention for sending news and messages, to a longer or shorter distance, by means of electricity, which is sent along wires that are suspended on poles.

*Q.* Describe a Fort.

*A.* A Fort is a large earthwork, building, or walled enclosure, defended by cannon.

*Q.* Describe a Lighthouse.

*A.* A Lighthouse is generally a lofty circular tower of great strength, erected on a dangerous coast or shore, or on rocks off the sea coast, from the top of which a strong bright light shines over the water at night, to guide or warn sailors.

## EXAMINATION LESSON X.

### Size, Motion, and Measurement of the Earth.

*Q.* Of what size is the Earth?

*A.* It is about 8,000 miles straight through its centre, or diameter, and nearly 25,000 miles round its outside, or circumference.

*Q.* How many motions has the Earth?

*A.* Three : 1st, its daily motion on its own axis, or centre; 2nd, its yearly motion round the Sun; and 3rd, its continuous motion in the sky with all the other planets.

**Fig. 19.**

| 1 mile. | 1 mile. | 3 miles in length. | | |
|---|---|---|---|---|
| 1 m. sq., or 1 sq.m. | 1 m. sq., or 1 sq.m. | 1 m. sq., or 1 sq.m. | 1 m. sq., or 1 sq.m. | 1 m. sq., or 1 sq.m. |
| 1 m. sq., or 1 sq.m. | 1 m. sq., or 1 sq.m. | 1 m. sq., or 1 sq.m. | 1 m. sq., or 1 sq.m. | 1 m. sq., or 1 sq.m. |
| 2 m. sq., or 4 sq. m. | | 6 square miles. | | |

*Q.* How is the extent of a country measured?

*A.* By miles of length and breadth, by square miles, and by miles square.

*Q.* What is a mile in length?

*A.* The distance, in a straight line, between any two points or places, as shown in Fig. 18.

*Q.* What is a mile square, or a square mile?

*A.* A square piece of country every side of which is a mile in length. (See Figs. 18, 19, & 20.)

*Q.* What are square miles?

*A.* A piece of country containing a number of miles square together, as shown in Figs. 18, 19, and 20.

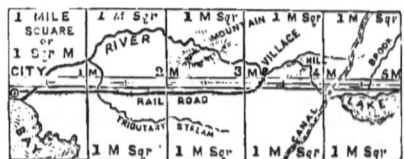

[Fig. 20.—A PIECE OF COUNTRY 5 MILES IN LENGTH BY 2 WIDE, MAKING 10 SQUARE MILES.

## EXAMINATION LESSON XI.*

### Imaginary Lines on the Surface of the Earth and in the Heavens.

*Q.* Describe the Axis of the Earth.

*A.* The axis of the Earth is an imaginary line passing from north to south, through its very centre.

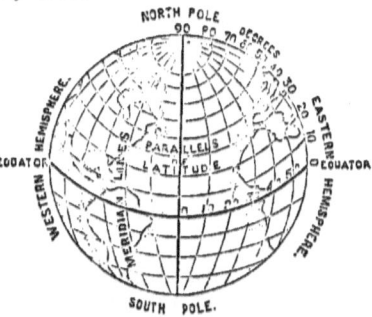

Fig. 21.—AXIS, POLES, GREAT AND LESS CIRCLES.

*Q.* What are the North and South Poles?

*A.* The precise points on the Earth's surface, at the north and south, where the Earth's axis terminates.

*Q.* What is the Equator?

*A.* A line running round the Earth at an equal distance from the North and South Poles.

*Q.* What are the Meridians?

*A.* Lines passing round the Earth through the North and South Poles.

*Q.* What is a first meridian?

*A.* A line running from north to south on the Earth's surface, through any particular place fixed upon by astronomers.

*Q.* Do you know of any such places fixed upon?

*A.* Yes: Greenwich [grin-idj], near London, in England; Paris, in France; and Washington, in the United States.

---

* This lesson, following in its natural order, should have preceded Lesson V. It was deemed desirable however rather to familiarize the mind of the pupil, at that stage, with the appearance of the Earth as it is actually seen by him, than to confuse him with a lesson on the imaginary lines on its surface, which cannot be seen at all. The lesson was therefore transferred to this place.

*Q. What is the use of a first meridian-line?*

*A.* To calculate the distance in degrees east or west from such first meridian-line to any other place on the Earth's surface.

*Q. What is Longitude?*

*A.* The distance in degrees of any place lying east or west from the first meridian-line.

*Q. What is Latitude?*

*A.* The distance in degrees from the Equator to any place north or south of it.

*Q. What are Parallels of Latitude?*

*A.* Lines of latitude running parallel to the Equator.

*Q. Where are degrees of latitude and of longitude marked on a map?*

*A.* Degrees of latitude are marked in figures on the right and left hand sides of a map; and degrees of longitude, at the top and bottom.

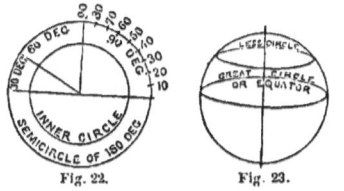

Fig. 22.        Fig. 23.

DEGREES, CIRCLES, ETC.

*Q. What is a Geographical Degree?*

*A.* A Geographical Degree is one of the three hundred and sixty equal parts into which every circle, whether large or small, is divided.

*Q. How many degrees are there from the Equator to either Pole?*

*A.* Ninety; that is, one fourth of a circle.

*Q. What is a Minute?*

*A.* The one-sixtieth part of a geographical degree. (A minute is also the one-sixtieth part of an hour.)

*Q. What is a Second?*

*A.* The one-sixtieth part of a minute.

*Q. Repeat the Astronomical Table.*

*A.* 60 Seconds (") make a Minute (').
60 Minutes make a Degree (°).
360 Degrees make a Circle (○).
30 Degrees make a Sign of the Zodiac.
3 Signs, or 90 Degrees, make a Quadrant (or one fourth) of the Zodiac.
12 Signs, or 4 Quadrants, or 360 Degrees, complete the circle of the Zodiac.

*Q. What is a Sign of the Zodiac?*

*A.* It is one of the twelve parts into which the Ancients divided the Zodiac.

*Q. Describe the Zodiac.*

*A.* The Zodiac is a space in the Heavens of eight degrees wide on each side of the ecliptic, within which all the planets perform their annual movements round the Sun.

*Q. Why was it called the Zodiac?*

*A.* Because the Ancients named its twelve parts chiefly after some animal,—and *zo-di-on* is the Greek word for a "little animal."

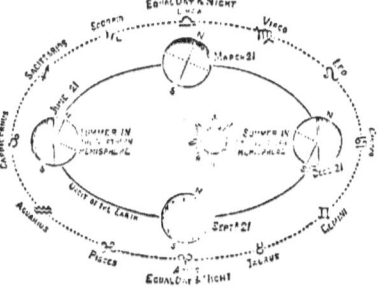

Fig. 24.—THE ZODIAC, WITH THE POSITION OF THE EARTH IN EACH OF THE FOUR SEASONS.

*Q. Name the twelve signs of the Zodiac, as shown in the engraving.*

*A.* 1. A-rī-es, the Ram.
2. Tau-rus, the Bull.
3. Gemini [jem'-ĭ-nī], the Twins.
4. Can-cer, the Crab.
5. Le-o, the Lion.
6. Vir-go, the Virgin.
7. Li-bra, the Balance.
8. Scor-pi-o, the Scorpion.
9. Sag-it-tā-ri-us [sadj-], the Archer.
10. Cap-ri-cor-nus, the Goat.
11. Aquarius [ä-kwā-rī-us], the Water-bearer.
12. Pis-cēs, the Fishes.

*Q. What is an Orbit?*

*A.* The path or course of any planet or other celestial body in the Heavens.

*Q. Describe the Ecliptic.*

*A.* The Ecliptic is the *apparent* path of the Sun in the Heavens, but it is *really* the path of the Earth round the Sun.

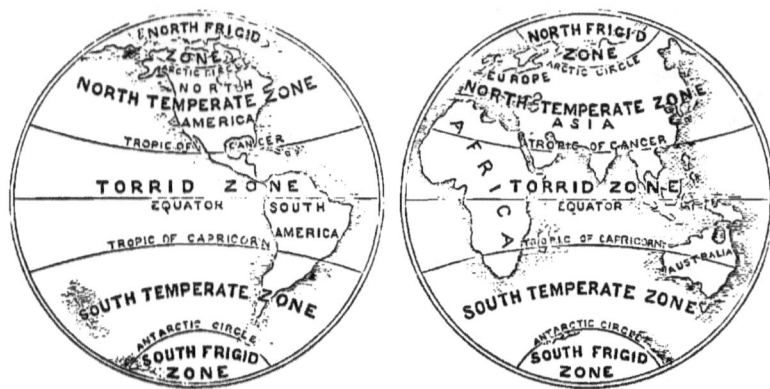

Fig. 25.—THE ZONES, TROPICS, AND CIRCLES.

Q. Why is it called the Ecliptic?

A. Because the eclipse, or partial darkening or hiding of the Sun or Moon from our view, takes place in or near it.

Q. Describe the Arctic and Antarctic or Polar Circles.

A. They are two circles round the Earth; one being about 23½ degrees from the North, and the other the same distance from the South Pole. (See Fig. 25.)

Q. Point them out in Fig. 25.

Q. Name the Tropics.

A. The Tropic of Cancer and the Tropic of Capricorn.

Q. Describe them, and point them out on Fig. 25.

A. They are two circles running parallel to the Equator, one being about 23½ degrees north, and the other the same distance south    it.

Fig. 26.—THE ZENITH, HORIZON, ETC.

Q. What are the Zones?

A. The Zones are belts passing round the Earth at equal distances from the Equator, and parallel to it.

Q. How many Zones are there?

A. The Tropics and the Polar Circles divide the Earth's surface into five Zones.

Q. Name them, and point them out on Fig. 25.

A. (1) The Torrid Zone, lying within the Tropics; (2, 3) the North and South Temperate Zones, one lying at each side of the Torrid Zone; (4, 5) the North and South Frigid Zones, lying respectively between the Arctic and Antarctic Circles and the Poles.

Q. What are the Antipodes?

A. They are points on the Earth's surface which are diametrically opposite to each other.

Q. What is the Zenith?

A. The place directly over the head of the spectator, as in Fig. 26.

Q. What is the Nadir?

A. The point in the sky exactly opposite to the Zenith, and under the spectator.

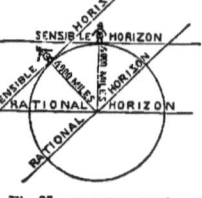

Fig. 27.—THE HORIZONS.

*Q.* Describe the Horizons.

*A.* The Sensible Horizon is where the Earth and the Sky appear to meet. The Rational Horizon is parallel to the Sensible, but 4,000 miles from it, as shown in Fig. 27.

---

# EXAMINATION LESSON XII.

## The Celestial or Heavenly Bodies.

*Q.* What celestial bodies revolve around the Sun?

*A.* The Planets, Comets, and Asteroids.

*Q.* What is a Planet?

*A.* A Planet (or "wanderer") is a heavenly body moving in a regular path or orbit.

*Q.* Why is it called a Planet?

*A.* To distinguish it from the Fixed Stars, which are supposed to be suns around which other planets, stars, &c., revolve.

*Q.* Do the Planets always maintain the same relative positions in the sky?

*A.* No: unlike the Fixed Stars, they are always slowly changing their places there.

*Q.* What is a Comet?

*A.* A heavenly body whose orbit is very eccentric,—that is, not nearly circular or round.

*Q.* What is the meaning of the word Comet?

*A.* "Comet" is from a Greek word meaning "hair," —so called from the long bright hair-like tail which generally accompanies it.

*Q.* What are Asteroids?

*A.* Asteroids are small bodies having the "form" of stars. They are also called Planetoids, because they have the "form" of planets.

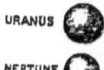

Fig. 28.—COMPARATIVE SIZES OF THE PLANETS.

*Q.* Name, in the order of their size, the principal Planets which revolve around the Sun.

*A.* Mer-cu-ry, Mars, Ve-nus, the Earth, Nep-tune, U'-ran-us, Sat-urn, and Ju-pi-ter.

*Q.* What are Moons, and how many has each planet?

*A.* Sat-el-lites, or "attendants," which revolve around the planets. Each planet has from one to eight moons attending it.

---

# EXAMINATION LESSON XIII.

## The World and its Inhabitants.

*Q.* Of what is the Earth's surface composed or made up?

*A.* Clay, sand, rocks, stones, and metals.

*Q.* Name some of the principal metals.

*A.* Gold, silver, copper, iron, lead, and tin.

*Q.* What grows out of the Earth's surface?

*A.* Trees, plants, grass, grain, vegetables, &c.

*Q.* What kinds of living creatures are found on it?

*A.* All kinds of tame and wild beasts, birds, reptiles, and insects.

*Q.* Does anything live in the waters of the Ocean?

*A.* Yes: all kinds of fish, including great whales.

*Q.* Can anything else but fish and whales live in the waters?

*A.* Yes: there are a great many birds, reptiles, and other animals that live partly in the water and partly on land.

*Q.* How was mankind scattered over the Earth?

*A.* A long time after Adam and Eve, our first parents, died, their children or descendants, who attempted to build the Tower of Babel, were scattered by God over "the face of all the Earth."—Genesis xi. 8.

*Q.* How are they now distinguished?

*A.* Their descendants who remained in Asia, are copper-coloured; those who moved into Europe, in course of time became white; and those who moved into Africa, became black.

---

# EXAMINATION LESSON XIV.

## Governments and Religions of the Earth.

*Q.* Do all the inhabitants of the World live in one country?

*A.* No: they live in different countries, and are divided into a great many nations.

*Q.* Are they all ruled by the same laws and under the same government?

*A.* No: each nation has its own laws and its own kind of government.

*Q.* What is the city or place called at which the laws are made?

*A.* The Capital, or Metropolis. (See Fig. 17.)

*Q. What are the names of the great national divisions of the Earth?*

*A.* Empires, Kingdoms, Republics, Duchies, and Principalities.

*Q. What is an Empire?*

*A.* One or more countries governed by an Emperor, Empress, or Sultan.

*Q. What is a Kingdom?*

*A.* One or more countries governed by a King or Queen.

*Q. What is the general name for rulers of this kind?*

*A.* Sov-*ereigns*, or Monarchs.

*Q. What is the general name for countries governed by this kind of rulers, and how are they distinguished?*

*A.* Mon-ar-chies [-kies]; and they are either Absolute or Con-sti-tu-tion-al [-shĕ-nal].

*Q. What is an Absolute Monarch?*

*A.* A monarch whose power is not limited by law, as in Russia or Turkey.

*Q. What is a Constitutional or Limited Monarch?*

*A.* A monarch whose power is limited by law, as in England.

*Q. What is a Republic?*

*A.* A country governed by a ruler called a President, who is elected for a certain number of years.

*Q. What are Duchies and Principalities?*

*A.* Countries governed by Dukes and Princes, who are either elective or hereditary.

*Q. What do you understand by hereditary government?*

*A.* A government in which the sovereignty descends to the son or heir of the last preceding ruler.

*Q. Are all the nations equally civilized?*

*A.* No: some are uncivilized, others are half-civilized, and the remainder are fully civilized.

*Q. How do nations become fully civilized?*

*A.* By means of the religion of the Bible, aided by education.

Fig. 29.—MANNER OF WORSHIP OR SYMBOLS OF THE DIFFERENT RELIGIONS.

*Q. Do all the nations of the World believe in the Christian religion?*

*A.* No: the Jews, the Mohammedans, and Pagans do not believe in it.

*Q. In what do the Jews believe?*

*A.* They believe in the Old, but not in the New Testament, and are still looking for a Messiah, or Saviour.

*Q. In what do the Mohammedans believe?*

*A.* They believe in the pretended revelations from Heaven of Mahomet (a religious impostor who lived in Arabia about 600 years after our Saviour's advent).

*Q. In what do Pagans, or Idolaters, believe?*

*A.* They believe in false gods, and worship idols made by their own hands.

*Q. In what do Christians believe?*

*A.* They "believe in GOD, the FATHER ALMIGHTY, maker of Heaven and Earth; in JESUS CHRIST, his only Son, our LORD"; and in "the HOLY GHOST, the Comforter." They believe also in the Bible, as GOD's word,—through which "holy men of old spake as they were moved by the HOLY GHOST."

## CONVERSATION VII.

### Conversational Trip through North America.

[Before learning the Geography of each country in N. America, we shall make a rapid trip over the whole of it.]

1. And first, before commencing our trip, we wish to tell our young friends that the Northmen, chiefly from Norway, are supposed to have discovered, by way of Iceland, the northern part of America about 800 years since. Christopher Columbus, who re-discovered America, sailed from Spain nearly 400 years ago, and on his first voyage across the Atlantic Ocean landed on one of the West-India Islands; but he did not reach the continent itself until two years afterwards.

2. One of the companions of Columbus, named A-mer-ĭ-cus Ves-pu-cĭ-us, wrote, after his return to Spain, an account of this discovery of the New World, and the country thus described came by degrees to be known as America.

3. After farther exploration on the new continent, it was found that it consisted of two great parts, which were afterward called North and South America. They are connected by the narrow isthmus of Dä-rĭ-en, or Pan-ä-ma [-mah].

4. Shortly after Columbus, Sir John Că-bot, who discovered British North America, sailed from England, and reached an island off the coast of America, which he called Newfoundland.

5. Leaving this island, we sail up the Gulf and River St. Lawrence, the Lakes Ou-tä-rĭ-o, E-rie, Hu-ron, and Superior, to Lake Win-nĭ-peg. From this lake we proceed along the Sas-katch-ë-wan river to the Rocky Mountains; beyond which are British Co-lum-bĭ-ä, Vancouver [van-koo-ver] Island, and the great Pacific Ocean.

6. Sailing up the Pacific coast, we pass Russian America, and then round it into the Arctic Ocean. Passing on through this region of ice and snow, we see many islands and other places (which have become famous from the search which was made among them for the celebrated English Arctic explorer Sir J. Franklin), and enter Baffin's Bay and Davis' Strait.

7. On one side we see Greenland, and on the other side, Lab-ră-dor. West of Labrador is a great inland sea called Hudson Bay. Passing down Davis' Strait, we again reach Newfoundland.

8. Sailing to the south, we pass Nova Scotia and reach the United States. Down this coast we see the Ber-mu-dä Isles, nearly opposite Cape Hat-të-ras, in North Carolina. We soon reach the Bä-hä-mä Islands and Flor-ĭ-dä, and pass into the Gulf of Mexico.

9. From this Gulf we sail up the noble Mississippi river, touch at New Orleans, and pass on to the far north. If we branch off near St. Louis and follow up the Missouri river, we can once more cross the Rocky Mountains and reach the Pacific Ocean again.

10. Sailing down the Pacific coast, we pass Or-ë-gon, Cal-ĭ-for-nĭ-ä, and Mexico, till we reach Central America. Crossing it, we reach the Ca-rib-be-an Sea; and just before us lie Jamaica, Cuba, Hayti, Porto Rico, and other well-known West-India Islands,—one of which was reached by Christopher Columbus when he discovered the New World. (See map of WEST INDIES, page 45.) Thus we end our rapid trip.

## EXAMINATION LESSON XV.

### Continent of America.

*Q. When and by whom was America discovered?*

*A.* By the Northmen, about 800 years ago; and by Christopher Columbus, in October 1492.

*Q. How did the new continent receive the name of America?*

*A.* It was named after Americus Vespucius, who wrote an account of the voyage of Columbus to the New World.

*Q. Name the two great divisions of America.*

*A.* North America and South America.

*Q. By what are they connected?*

*A.* By the isthmus of Durien, or Panama. (See WESTERN HEMISPHERE, page 8.)

PRINCIPAL ANIMALS ON THE CONTINENT OF AMERICA.

## EXAMINATION LESSON XVI.

### North America.

*Q.* Point out and name the principal animals on the Continent of America, as shown in the engraving.

*A.* 1, the Wolf; 2, Fox; 3, Otter; 4, Bear; 5, Moose; 6, Llama; 7, Buffalo (or, more correctly, the Bison); 8, 9, Beaver; 10, Wild Horse; 11, Condor; 12, Alligator.

*Q.* Trace on the map the trip just made.

*Q.* Point out on the map the boundaries of North America.

*Q.* Point out and name the chief divisions of North America.

*A.* Greenland, or Danish [day-nish] America; Russian [rush-an] America; British America; the United States; Mexico; Central America; and the West-India Islands.

*Q.* Point out and name the great mountain-ranges in North America.

*A.* The Rocky Mountains, on the Pacific coast; and the Alleghany [al-lĕ-gay-në] Mountains, on the Atlantic coast.

*Q.* Point out and name the principal lakes.

*A.* Ontario, Erie, Huron, Michigan [mish-ĕ-gan'], Superior, Winnipeg, Ath-ă-bas-că, Great Slave, and Great-Bear Lakes.

*Q.* Point out and name the great rivers.

*A.* The St. Lawrence to the east, the Mississippi to the south, and the Mackenzie to the north.

*Q.* Point out and name the other principal rivers.

*A.* Ottawa, Ohio, Rio Gran-de, Missouri, Saskatchewan, Columbia, and Kwickpack.

*Q.* Point out and name the oceans.

*A.* The Atlantic, Pacific, and Arctic Oceans.

*Q.* Point out and name the great bays at the north.

*A.* Baffin's and Hudson Bays.

*Q.* Point out and name the principal gulfs.

*A.* St. Lawrence, Mexico, and California.

*Q.* Point out and name the principal straits.

*A.* Davis, Belle-Isle, and Yu-că-tan Channel, along the east coast.

*Q.* Point out and name the principal islands.

*A.* Parry, Melville; Banks, Albert, and Victoria Land; Booth-ī-ă, Cockburn [ko-burn], Cumberland, and Southampton, at the north; Newfoundland, Cape Bret-on, Long Island;

**NORTH AMERICA**
English Miles.
Eng? for Easy Lessons in Gen? Geog?

the Bermudă, Ba-hä-mă, and other islands of the West Indies, off the east coast; Vancouver and Queen-Charlotte's, off the west coast.

Q. Point out and name the principal capes.

A. Farewell, Charles, Race, Breton, Sable Cod, May, Hatteras; Ca-toche [-tosh], Gra_ cias-a-Dios [grä'-se-ass-ŭ-dee'-oce], Cor-ri-en-tes, St. Lucas, Men-do-ci-no [-se-no], Blanco; Flattery, Barrow, &c.

*Q.* Point out and name the chief peninsulas.

*A.* Greenland, Labrador, Nova Scotia, Florida, Yucatan, California, and Russian America.

---

### EXAMINATION LESSON XVII.

#### Russian, Danish, and French North America.

*Q.* Point out on the map the position and boundaries of Russian America.

*Q.* Name, and point out on the map, its river and cape.

*A.* The River Kwickpack and Cape Barrow.

*Q.* What countries are included in Danish America?

*A.* The peninsula of Greenland, and the island of Iceland. (See W. HEMISPHERE, p. 8.)

*Q.* Point out their position on the map.

*Q.* Point out on the map of Newfoundland, and name, the French islands.

*A.* Miquelon and Langley; capital, St. Pierre.

*Q.* What is the occupation of their inhabitants?

*A.* Cod-fishing, and drying the fish for export.

---

### EXAMINATION LESSON XVIII.

#### Hudson-Bay Territory.

*Q.* Point out on the map of North America the position of the vast territory around Hudson Bay.

*Q.* After whom was this territory named?

*A.* After Henry Hudson, an Englishman, who discovered the bay about 250 years ago.

*Q.* For what is it chiefly noted?

*A.* For the valuable furs of its wild animals, and its numerous rivers.

*Q.* Point out and name those rivers.

*A.* Great Whale river, Red river, Saskatchewan river, and Mackenzie river.

*Q.* What places lie to the south between James Bay and the Rocky Mountains?

*A.* Various trading-posts; the principal one of which is the Red-River Settlement.

*Q.* For what are these areas of country chiefly noted?

*A.* For their fertile soil, and rich coal-fields.

*Q.* Name and point out the principal rivers and lakes in these settlements.

*Q.* What country lies between Hudson Bay and Newfoundland?

*A.* Labrador, a cold country, but with valuable fisheries off the coast.

---

### EXAMINATION LESSON XIX.

#### British Columbia and Vancouver Island.

*Q.* How can you reach British Columbia from the Upper Saskatchewan river?

*A.* Through several passes, or openings, in the Rocky Mountains.

*Q.* Point out the position of British Columbia.

*Q.* Name and point out its principal rivers.

*Q.* For what is it chiefly noted?

*A.* For its rich gold-fields.

*Q.* Name and point out the capital.

*A.* New Westminster, near the mouth of the Fraser river.

*Q.* Point out on the map the position and boundaries of Vancouver Island.

*Q.* Point out its straits, gulfs, &c.

*Q.* For what is it chiefly noted?

*A.* For being the largest island on the Pacific coast, and for its fisheries, coal, and furs.

*Q.* Name and point out its capital.

*A.* Victoria, at the south of the island.

---

### EXAMINATION LESSON XX.

#### British North America.

*Q.* Point out on the map of North America, the boundaries of British North America.

*Q.* What ocean lies to the north?—to the east?—and to the west?

*A.* The Arctic Ocean to the north, the Atlantic to the east, and the Pacific to the west.

*Q.* What great bay lies north of Canada?

*A.* Hudson Bay.

*Q.* What smaller bay lies between Hudson Bay and Canada?

*A.* James Bay.

*Q.* What bay and strait lie still farther to the north-east?

*A.* Baffin's Bay and Davis' Strait.

*Q.* What great range of mountains lies near the Pacific coast?

*A.* The Rocky Mountains.

Niagara river into Lakes Erie, St. Clair, and Huron; and at the Sault Ste. Marie [so-sant'-mă-ree'], enter Lake Superior; and thus reach the N. W. limits of Upper Canada.

## EXAMINATION LESSON XXI.

### Provinces of British North America.

*Q.* Trace on the map of the B.N.A. Provinces the trip we have just made.

*Q.* Point out on the same map the position of Newfoundland, Cape Breton, Nova Scotia, Prince-Edward Island, New Brunswick, Lower Canada, and Upper Canada.

*Q.* Point out on the map and name their capitals.

*Q.* Point out and name the other large cities.

*Q.* How many of these Provinces touch upon the coast?

*A.* All of them but Upper Canada.

*Q.* Name and point out the chief rivers and lakes.

*Q.* Between which two lakes do the Niagara Falls occur?

*A.* Between Lakes Erie and Ontario.

*Q.* What country and bay lie north of Upper Canada?

*A.* Prince-Rupert Land and James Bay.

*Q.* What bay lies west of Upper Canada?

*A.* Georgian Bay, east of Lake Huron.

*Q.* Which of the United States lie south of Canada?

*Q.* What islands lie in the Gulf of St. Lawrence?

*A.* Anticosti, Magdalen, Prince Edward, Cape-Breton, and Newfoundland.

*Q.* Name and point out the bays, capes, and straits.

## CONVERSATION VIII.

### Conversational Trip through the Provinces of British North America.

1. From the island of Newfoundland, we sail a little to the south and touch at Cape-Breton Island, and then reach Prince-Edward Island; south of which we see an isthmus which joins Nova Scotia to New Brunswick.

2. Touching at the Magdalen Islands, and sailing up the Gulf of St. Lawrence, we see before us Anticosti island and the coast of Labrador. Turning to the left hand, we enter the noble Canadian river St. Lawrence, —so called by its discoverer, Jacques Cartier.

3. Proceeding up this river, we sail past the mouth of the Sag-ue-nay and reach Quebec. We then pass the river St. Mau-rice, and arrive at Montreal, on the island of that name. At the head of this island, we see the river Ottawa, which separates Upper from Lower Canada. Still sailing up the St. Lawrence, we come to the boundary-line between Canada and the United States, and enter the beautiful Lake Ontario at Kingston. From Kingston we proceed to Toronto; and pass over from it to the magnificent Falls of Niagara,—one of the greatest wonders of the world.

4. From these Falls we pass rapidly up the

## CONVERSATION IX.

### Conversational Trip through Newfoundland.

1. If we follow the route of the Canadian steamers from Canada to Europe, we shall soon enter the Strait of Belle Isle,—so called from an island of that name north of Newfoundland.

2. Passing out of that strait, we turn to the south along the "Banks" until we reach Cape Freels and Cape Bonavista,—which latter cape is supposed to have been the land first

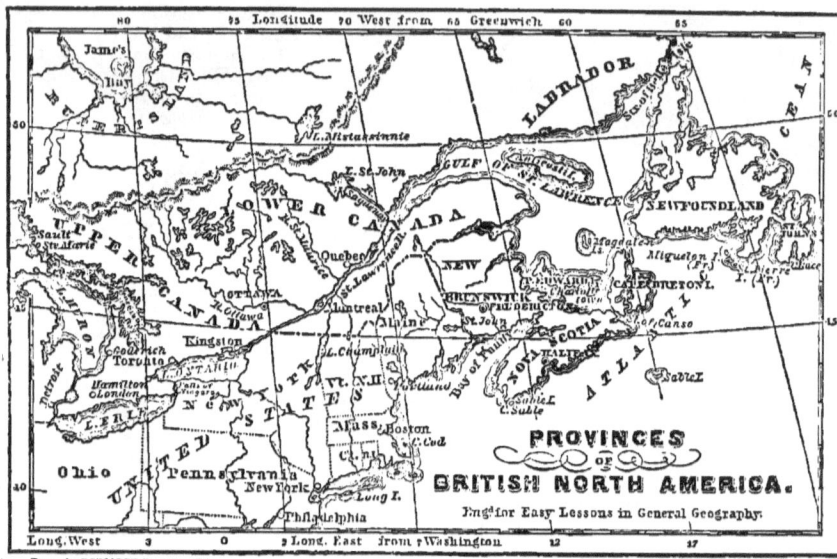

seen by Sir John Cabot when he discovered the island.

3. Farther on, we come to St. Johns, the capital of the island, situated on a peninsula indented with several deep bays. Rounding this peninsula by way of Cape Race and going westward, we touch at the islands of French North America.

APPEARANCE OF NEWFOUNDLAND FROM A BALLOON.

4. From this point round by Cape Ray to the Strait of Belle Isle, the coast is but little inhabited, except by fishermen, who land to dry their fish. The interior contains several ponds or lakes. A telegraph-line, by way of Cape Ray, connects Newfoundland with Nova Scotia.

---

### EXAMINATION LESSON XXII.
—
#### Newfoundland Island.

Q. Trace on the map the trip just made.

Q. Point out on the map the position and boundaries of Newfoundland.

Q. What countries lie north-west of the island?

A. Labrador and Canada.

Q. Point out on the map and name its bays and capes.

Q. Point out and name its ponds or lakes, and rivers.

Q. Point out and name its district-divisions.

Q. For what is Newfoundland chiefly noted?

A. For its valuable coast-fisheries, and for being the first-settled British-American Colony.

*Q.* What is peculiar about Newfoundland?

*A.* The fogs on the coast, and the great sand-banks at the S. and E. of the island.

*Q.* Point out on the map the course of the telegraph between St. Johns and Nova Scotia, by way of Cape Ray.

*Q.* What strait lies at the north of the island?

*A.* The Strait of Belle-Isle,—through which

the Canadian mail-steamers pass, in the summer season, on their way to and from Europe.

*Q.* Point out and name the capital of Newfoundland.

*A.* St. Johns, at the south-east of the island.

## CONVERSATION X.

### Conversational Trip through Prince-Edward Island.

From Newfoundland we proceed in a south-
westerly direction to Prince-Edward Island.
As we go round the coast of this island, we see
that it is crescent-shaped. We also notice that
two deep bays cut the island nearly into three
parts. Near Hillsborough Bay we find Charlottetown, the capital.

## EXAMINATION LESSON XXIII.

### Prince-Edward Island.

*Q.* Point out on the map of Nova Scotia, the position
and boundaries of Prince-Edward Island.

*Q.* What countries lie to the S. E. and S. W. of it?

*A.* Cape-Breton Island, Nova Scotia, and
New Brunswick.

*Q.* Point out and name its principal bays and capes.

*Q.* Name and point out its county-divisions.

*A.* King's, Queen's, and Prince counties

*Q.* For what is the island chiefly noted?

*A.* For its fertility and its healthy climate.

*Q.* Name and point out the strait at the south.

*Q.* Point out and name its capital.

*A.* Charlottetown, near Hillsborough Bay.

## CONVERSATION XI.

### Conversational Trip through Nova Scotia and Cape-Breton Island.

1. From Prince-Edward Island, we sail
across Northumberland Strait to Bay Verte,
on the north-west coast of Nova Scotia. From
this we go eastward, passing Pic-tou [-ton]
and Cape St. George, and cross St. George's Bay.

2. From Port Hood we sail north-east along
the coast of Cape-Breton Island till we reach
Cape North. Rounding it, we follow the coast

APPEARANCE OF NOVA SCOTIA, ETC., FROM A BALLOON.

and explore Bras-d'Or Lake, and pass Sydney,
the capital.

3. As we reach the Atlantic Ocean, we turn
to the south-west along the coast, passing Cape
Canso; until we reach Halifax, the capital of
Nova Scotia, with its fine and spacious harbour
and well-fortified citadel.

4. From Halifax, we go on to Cape Sable;
where we round the peninsula and turn to the
north-west into the Bay of Fundy. We find
the upper end of this bay divided by the Cobequid mountains into Mi-nas or Mi-nes
Channel and Chiegnecto Bay.

5. At Windsor, in Hants County, south of
Minas Basin, we can take the railway for Halifax. From Halifax we proceed along another
line of railway to Truro, and from it on till
we reach Bay Verte again.

## EXAMINATION LESSON XXIV.

### Nova Scotia and Cape-Breton Island.

*Q.* Trace on the map the trip just made.

*Q.* Point out on the map the position and boundaries
of the Province of Nova Scotia and Cape-Breton Island.

*Q.* What islands lie north of Nova Scotia?

*A.* Prince-Edward and Cape-Breton.

*Q.* To what Province is Nova Scotia connected by an
isthmus?

*A.* To New Brunswick, at the north-west.

*Q.* Name and point out the principal harbours.

*Q.* Point out and name their principal bays and capes.

*Q.* What is peculiar about the Bay of Fundy?

*A.* It is generally very stormy, and its tides
sometimes rise 60 feet high.

Q. For what are Nova Scotia and Cape-Breton noted?

A. For their coal, iron, and other minerals; and for their extensive coast, and good harbours.

Q. What separates Cape-Breton from Nova Scotia?

A. The "Gut" or Strait of Canso.

Q. Name and point out the principal islands.

*Q.* Name and point out the principal lakes, rivers, and mountains.

*Q.* Name and point out the county-divisions on the Atlantic coast,—on the Bay of Fundy,—and on Northumberland Strait.

*Q.* What chief places do the lines of railway connect?

*A.* Halifax with Windsor and Truro.

*Q.* Name and point out the capital of Cape-Breton Isl.

*A.* Sydney, in Cape-Breton County.

*Q.* Name and point out the capital and principal towns of Nova Scotia.

*A.* Halifax, the capital, in Halifax County; Pictou, at the north; Truro, at the head of Cobequid Bay; Windsor, in Hants County; Liverpool, in Queen's County; and Lunenburg, in Lunenburg County.

*Q.* What group of islands lies north of Prince-Edward Island?

*A.* The Magdalen Islands, which belong to Canada.

---

## CONVERSATION XII.
### —
### Conversational Trip through New Brunswick.

1. If we enter New Brunswick from Nova Scotia, we proceed along the projected railway-line to Shediac, thence along the coast to Richibucto Harbour and Miramichi Bay, and round by Shippegan Island into the Bay of Chaleurs.

2. Sailing up this bay for some distance, we reach the mouth of the Res-ti-gouche [-goosh] river, which, with the bay, forms the boundary between Canada and New Brunswick. Leaving this river, we travel southward across the country to the Grand Falls of the St. John river.

3. From these falls, we descend this fine river to Fredericton, the capital, or seat of government. Leaving Fredericton, we soon arrive at St. John, the commercial capital of the Province, at the mouth of the St. John river.

4. We now follow the coast-line along the Bay of Fundy, and reach the head of Chiegnecto Bay. From Amherst we come to Bay Verte, and thence go round by Shediac.

5. Returning by railway to St. John, and from that city to the head of Passamaquoddy Bay, we pass down among the islands to the Great Manan. Returning from it by St.

Stephen, we proceed by railway up to Woodstock, passing the picturesque Grand Lake to the left on the boundary-line. [We should remember that there is another Grand Lake, connected with the St. John river, in Queen's County.] From Woodstock we sail up the St. John until we again reach the boundary-line of Canada.

---

## EXAMINATION LESSON XXV.
### —
### New Brunswick.

*Q.* Trace on the map the trip just made.

*Q.* Point out on the map the position and boundaries of New Brunswick.

*Q.* What large bay separates New Brunswick from Canada?

*A.* The Bay of Chaleurs, at the north.

*Q.* Point out and name its other bays and harbours.

*Q.* Point out and name the principal islands.

*Q.* What counties lie on the Bay of Chaleurs?—on the Gulf of St. Lawrence and Northumberland Strait?—on the Bay of Fundy?—in the interior?—and on Maine boundary?

*Q.* For what is New Brunswick chiefly noted?

*A.* For its square shape, its many rivers, and its extensive ship-building.

*Q.* Name and point out its principal lakes?

*A.* Grand Lake in Queen's County, and Grand Lake on the Maine boundary.

*Q.* Which are its largest rivers?

*A.* The Restigouche, which falls into the Bay of Chaleurs; the Miramichi, which falls into Miramichi Bay; and the St. John, which falls into the Bay of Fundy.

*Q.* Point out and name the chief seaport.

*A.* St. John, at the mouth of St. John river.

*Q.* Point out and name the capital.

*A.* Fredericton, 84 miles up the St. John.

*Q.* Point out and name the chief towns along the coast.

---

## CONVERSATION XIII.
### —
### Conversational Trip through Lower Canada.

1. Leaving New Brunswick by the Restigouche river, and crossing to the Metis river (in Canada), we come to the river St. Lawrence.

2. Turning to the south-west, we gradually

NEW
BRUNSWICK
Engraved for Easy Lessons in Gen. Geog.

reach the mouth of the Saguenay river, to the right. Up this fine river we can go in a ship for 75 miles; and from its source we can soon reach overland the head-waters of the St. Maurice river. Passing down the St. Maurice, we enter the St. Lawrence again, at Three Rivers ;

3. But leaving it and passing up the St. Lawrence, we come to the island of Orleans; beyond which we see before us, the famous citadel of Quebec, commanding the city.

4. As we leave Quebec, the river becomes narrower till we reach the city of Three Rivers, situated at the three-fold mouth of the St. Maurice river; a short distance below the foot of Lake St. Peter, which is an expansion of the St. Lawrence. Soon we come within sight of the stirring city of Montreal, and its cele-

THE VICTORIA TUBULAR RAILWAY-BRIDGE, FROM ST. LAMBERT.

brated Victoria Bridge. This bridge is nearly two miles long. It is built of iron, and shaped like a square tube or tunnel, through which the railway-trains run with safety.

5. If we prefer it, we can also go to Montreal by railway. Leaving Point Levi, opposite Quebec, we come to Richmond; and thence, through St. Hyacinthe, a flourishing city, to Montreal. At Richmond we could also go on direct, through the Eastern Townships, passing Sherbrooke, their chief town, to Portland.

### EXAMINATION LESSON XXIV.

#### Lower Canada.

*Q.* Trace on the map the trip just made.

*Q.* Point out the position & boundaries of Lower Canada.

*Q.* Which is its largest river?

*A.* The St. Lawrence, which flows northeast into the Gulf of the same name.

*Q.* Name the principal rivers north of the St. Lawrence.

*A.* The Saguenay, St. Maurice, and Ottawa.

*Q.* Name the principal rivers south of the St. Lawrence.

*A.* The Richelieu, St. Francis, and Chaudière.

*Q.* For what is Lower Canada noted?

*A.* For its shipping, fisheries, iron and copper mines, and its beautiful scenery.

*Q.* What peninsula lies to the north-east?

*A.* Gaspé; lying between the Gulf of St. Lawrence and the Bay of Chaleurs.

*Q.* Name and point out the principal counties.

*Q.* Name and point out the cities.

*A.* Quebec, Three Rivers, Montreal, and St. Hyacinthe.

*Q.* Point out and name the capital.

*A.* Quebec, noted for its celebrated fortress.

*Q.* What celebrated iron railway-bridge crosses the St. Lawrence at Montreal?

*A.* The Victoria Bridge, which is shaped like a tube or tunnel, and is nearly two miles long.

*Q.* Name the chief town in the Eastern Townships?

*A.* Sherbrooke, on the rivers St. Francis and Magog.

*Q.* What railway connects Quebec and Montreal with Portland in the State of Maine?

*A.* The Grand Trunk Railway, which extends to Lake Huron in Upper Canada.

*Q.* Which are the principal islands in the St. Lawrence?

*A.* Montreal, and Isle Jesus, at Montreal; Orleans, at Quebec; and Anticosti, in the Gulf.

### CONVERSATION XIV.

#### Conversational Trip through Upper Canada.

1. Leaving Montreal by the Ottawa river, we reach Ottawa City, the new capital of Canada. On our way up we see on the right several rivers flowing into the Ottawa.

2. We can also proceed to Upper Canada by the St. Lawrence, passing many flourishing towns and villages on our way. The rapids on this river are beautiful; so also is the scenery among the Thousand Islands, near Kingston.

3. At Kingston we enter Lake Ontario; proceeding up which, we pass Cobourg, Port Hope, and Whitby, before we come to Toronto.

4. From Toronto we cross the lake to the

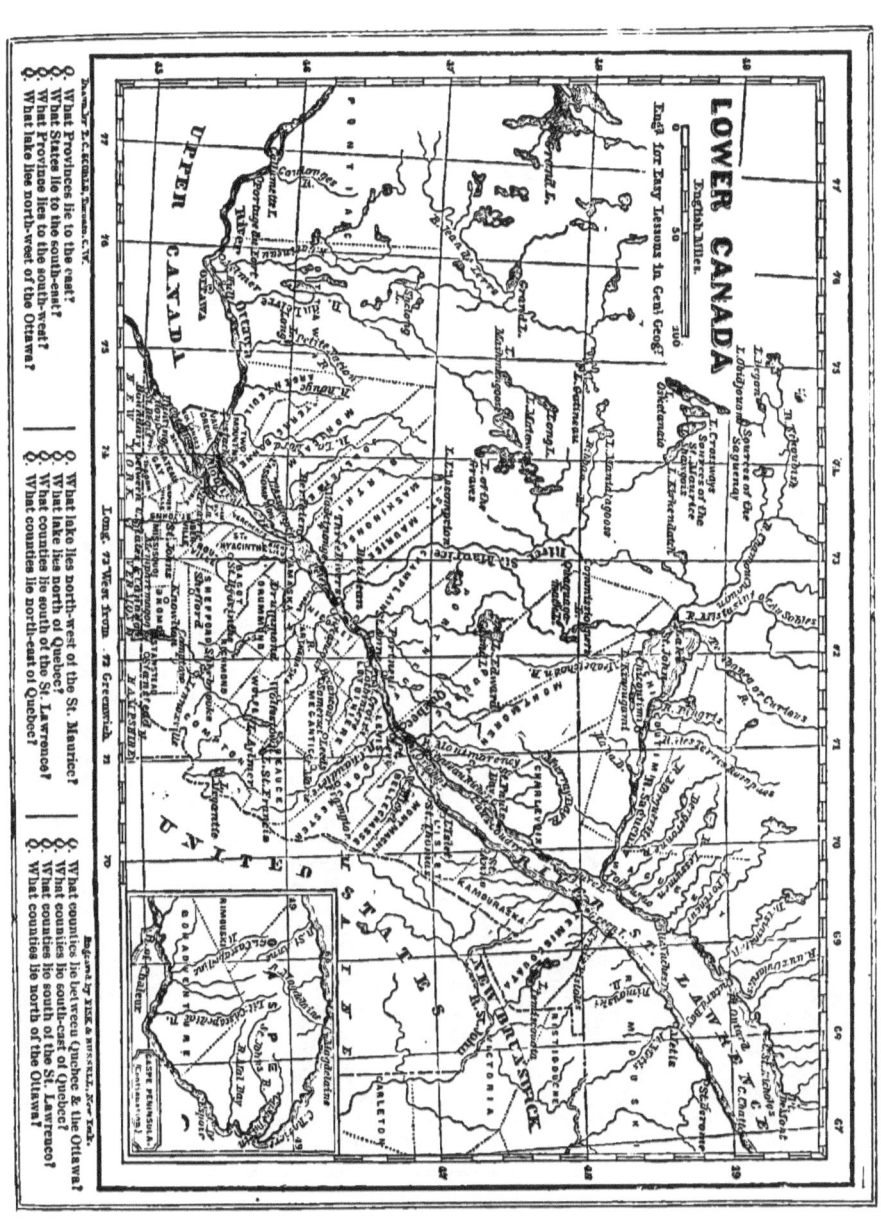

LOWER CANADA

English Miles.

Eng? for Easy Lessons in Gen! Geog?

Long. 73 West from 72 Greenwich 71

Pub. by D. C. KOLLAR, Toronto, C.W.

Engraved by FISK & RUSSELL, New York.

◊◊◊ What Provinces lie to the east?
◊◊◊ What States lie to the south-east?
◊◊◊ What Province lies to the south-west?
◊◊◊ What lake lies north-west of the Ottawa?

◊◊◊ What lake lies north-west of the St. Maurice?
◊◊◊ What lake lies north of Quebec?
◊◊◊ What counties lie south-east of Quebec?
◊◊◊ What counties lie south of the St. Lawrence?

◊◊◊ What counties lie between Quebec & the Ottawa?
◊◊◊ What counties lie south-east of Quebec?
◊◊◊ What counties lie south of the St. Lawrence?
◊◊◊ What counties lie north of the Ottawa?

celebrated Falls of Niagara; thence we go westward to St. Catherines, Hamilton, Paris, Brantford, Woodstock, London, St. Thomas, and Chatham, and enter Lake St. Clair.

5. From Lake St. Clair, we go northward, past Sarnia, into Lake Huron. Thence, touching at Goderich, we coast along the County of Bruce peninsula to the island of Manitoulin, and to the Bruce Mines; and so on to Sault Ste. Marie, at the entrance of Lake Superior.

6. Retracing our steps, we enter the Georgian Bay; and reaching Collingwood, we proceed to Barrie and Lake Simcoe. At Beaverton we cross over to the group of lakes in the Counties of Victoria, Peterboro', Northumberland, and Hastings, till we come to the river Moira, at the mouth of which is Belleville.

7. From Belleville we pass down the beautiful Bay of Quinté, north of Prince-Edward County, till we reach Kingston again.

### EXAMINATION LESSON XXV.

#### Upper Canada.

*Q.* Trace on the map the trip just made.

*Q.* Point out the boundaries of Upper Canada.

*Q.* Point out and name each of the great lakes.

*Q.* What river separates Upper from Lower Canada?

*A.* The Ottawa, which falls into the St. Lawrence at the island of Montreal.

*Q.* Point out the other boundary-rivers of Upper Canada.

*A.* The Niagara, Detroit, and St. Clair.

*Q.* What bays lie north of Grey and Simcoe Counties?

PROPOSED PARLIAMENT-BUILDINGS, OTTAWA.

*Q.* What lakes lie between the Ottawa river and Georgian Bay?

*Q.* What rivers flow into Georgian Bay?

*Q.* What rivers flow into Lake St. Clair?

*Q.* Point out the Madawaska river.

*Q.* What peninsulas separate Lake Erie from Lake Ontario, Lake Erie from Lake St. Clair, and Lake Erie from Georgian Bay.

*Q.* Point out and name the cities of Upper Canada.

*A.* London, Hamilton, Toronto, Kingston, and Ottawa.

*Q.* Point out and name the chief towns on the map.

*Q.* For what is Upper Canada chiefly noted?

*A.* For its great lakes, fertile soil, and agricultural products; its copper, iron, and other minerals; and its oil-springs.

### CONVERSATION XV.

#### Conversational Sketch of the Queen.

1. All good and loyal little boys and girls will no doubt like to hear something about our dearly loved Queen. When she is addressed in writing by her subjects she is styled Her Most Gracious Majesty Queen Victoria; but she is generally called The Queen. Before she was a queen, she was called the Princess Victoria.

2. The Queen lives in England, where she has several beautiful palaces, in different parts of the country. In London a number of wise and distinguished men assist her in governing her great empire.

3. Among the Queen's forefathers were the celebrated Alfred the Great, and William the Conqueror. The King who reigned before our Queen was her uncle, William IV. When he died, she was made Queen of the whole British empire (including all the British colonies).

4. The Queen had an excellent mother, who early taught her to love GOD. When the Princess Victoria's uncle died and she was told that she was a queen, her first act was to kneel and pray to GOD for his divine guidance.

5. The Queen has ever since ruled the empire so wisely, that she is greatly beloved by all her subjects. She has a number of children, who, from their high rank, are called Princes and Princesses. Her eldest son, the Prince of Wales, visited the British North-American Provinces in 1860, and was welcomed with great love and affection by all classes of the people.

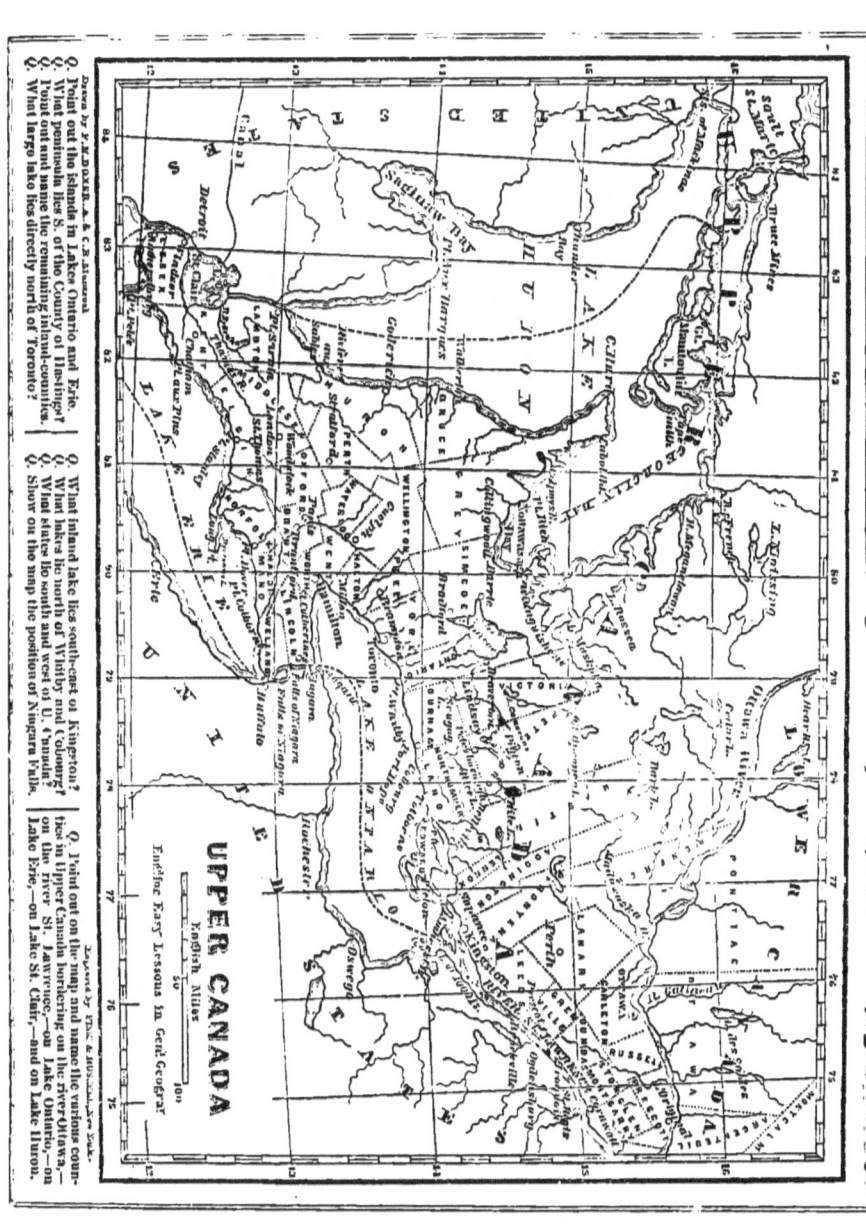

UPPER CANADA

English Miles

Twelve Easy Lessons in Gen'l Geograf'

HER MAJESTY QUEEN VICTORIA.

6. In 1861 the Queen suffered a great loss in the death of her noble husband, Prince Albert the good. All her subjects mourned with her, and from every part of her vast empire she received the warmest sympathy.

7. Our duty to the Queen is to love her, and to obey the laws of our country. The Bible says, "fear God and honor the King," and "obey them that have the rule over you." With one heart and voice, our prayers for her should continually ascend; and in the words of our National Anthem, we should all heartily sing:

"God save our gracious Queen,
  Long live our noble Queen!
    God save the Queen!
  Send her victorious,
  Happy and glorious,
  Long to reign over us!
    God save the Queen!"

## EXAMINATION LESSON XXVI.

### The Queen, and the Government of Canada.

Q. Give, in your own words, some account of the Queen.

Q. What is our duty towards the Queen?

A. The Bible teaches us, not only to "fear God," but to "honour the King," [Queen, or chief ruler.]

Q. How, then, should we act as dutiful subjects of the Queen?

A. We should be truly loyal to her as our Sovereign; and we should obey God's laws, as well as those of our country.

Q. Who represents the Queen in Canada?

A. His Excellency the Governor-General.

Q. By whom are the laws of Canada and England enacted?

A. In Canada by the Queen's Representative, with the advice and consent of the Legislative Council and House of Assembly; and in England by the Queen, with the consent of Parliament.

---

## CONVERSATION XVI.

### Conversational Trip through the United States of America.

1. Leaving Canada by the Grand Trunk Railway, we soon reach Portland, in the State of Maine. From that city we can go along the coast to Boston, the capital of Massachusetts; thence round Cape Cod to New York, which is the chief shipping-port of the United States.

2. From New York we go up the Hudson river to Albany, and thence to the great lakes; or still proceeding along the sea-coast, we pass Delaware Bay, some distance up which is Philadelphia. Farther to the south is the city of Washington, the capital of the Northern United States.

3. From Washington we proceed through Virginia, by way of Richmond (capital of the Southern Confederate States), to the ocean again. Going still farther south, we pass the States of North Carolina, South Carolina,

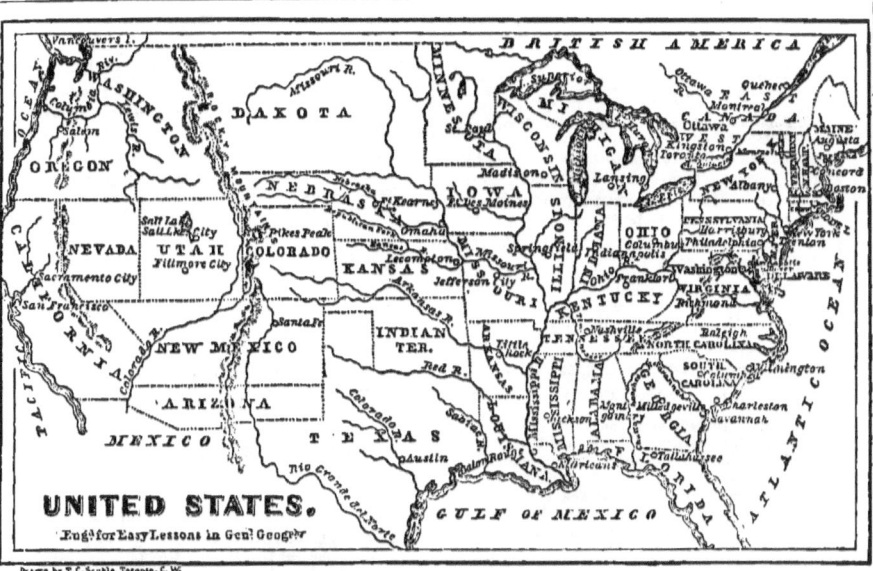

UNITED STATES.
Eng^d for Easy Lessons in Gen? Geog?

Drawn by T. C. Scuble, Toronto, C. W.

Georgia, and their commercial cities of Wilmington, Charleston, and Savannah, till we reach the peninsula of Florida. Going round Florida, we sail along the coasts of the States of Alabama, Mississippi, and Louisiana.

4. In Louisiana we enter the great Mississippi river; and going northward to its source, we pass, on the right hand, the States of Mississippi, Tennessee, Kentucky, Illinois, and Wisconsin. At Kentucky the Ohio river joins the Mississippi; along the northern banks of which are the States of Indiana and Ohio.

5. On the left-hand side of the Mississippi from its mouth, we pass the States of Louisiana, Arkansas, Missouri, Iowa, and Minnesota. Coming down the river again to Missouri, we turn westward up the Missouri river, passing the States of Kansas, Nebraska, and Dakotah, till we reach the Rocky Mountains.

6. Crossing these mountains, we enter Washington Territory, and pass into Oregon, Utah, Nevada, and California, on the Pacific coast.

7. From California we proceed eastward through New Mexico, Arizona, and Texas to the Gulf of Mexico; and thus end our trip.

---

## EXAMINATION LESSON XXVII.

### The United States of America.

Q. Trace on the map the trip just made.

Q. Point out on the map the position and boundaries of the United States of America.

Q. Point out the great chain of mountains which runs along the Atlantic coast.

Q. Point out the principal rivers in the United States.

A. The Ohio, Missouri, Arkansas, Mississippi, Colorado, and Columbia.

Q. Point out and name the principal bays.

Q. Point out and name the principal capes.

Q. How many States and Territories are there in the United States?

A. Thirty-six States and ten Territories.

Q. How are these States and Territories divided?

A. Into Eastern, Middle, Southern, and Western.

## EXAMINATION LESSON XXVIII.

### The New-England or Eastern States, and the Northern or Middle States.

*Q.* Point out and name the Eastern or New-England States, and their capitals.

*A.* MAINE, capital *Augusta;* NEW HAMP-SHIRE, capital *Concord;* VERMONT, capital *Montpelier;* MASSACHUSETTS, capital *Boston;* RHODE ISLAND, capitals *Providence* and *New-port;* and CONNECTICUT, capitals *Hartford* and *New Haven.*

*Q.* Point out and name the Middle or Northern States, and their capitals.

*A.* NEW YORK, capital *Albany;* PENNSYL-VANIA, capital *Harrisburg;* NEW JERSEY, capital *Trenton;* DELAWARE, capital *Dover.*

*Q.* What State lies between Canada and New Brunswick?

*Q.* What three States border on the State of New York?
*Q.* What State lies between Maine and Vermont?
*Q.* What two States lie south of Massachusetts?
*Q.* What two States border on the Canadian lakes?
*Q.* What two States lie south of New York? .
*Q.* What State lies south-west of New Jersey?
*Q.* What large island lies east of New Jersey?
*Q.* What mountains run through the New-England States?

*A.* The Alleghanies, which run southward.

*Q.* What are these mountains called in Vermont and in New Hampshire?

*A.* In Vermont they are called the Green Mountains; and in New Hampshire, the White Mountains.

*Q.* What mountains extend through the Middle States?
*Q.* Name the principal rivers in each State.
*Q.* Point out and name the capes and bays on the coast.
*Q.* What lake lies between Canada, New Hampshire, and Vermont?
*Q.* What bay separates Delaware from New Jersey?
*Q.* What river separates Pennsylvania from New Jersey?
*Q.* What river separates New York from New Jersey?

*A.* The Hudson, celebrated for its scenery.

*Q.* What important river takes its rise in Pennsylvania?

*A.* The Ohio, a tributary of the Mississippi.

*Q.* Which is the chief railway-centre in the New-England States?

*A.* Boston, the chief business city of New England.

*Q.* Which is the chief railway-centre in the Northern States?

*A.* New York, the commercial capital of the United States.

*Q.* For what are the New-England States chiefly noted?

*A.* For their early settlement by the English, and for their extensive manufactures.

*Q.* For what are the Northern States chiefly noted?

*A.* New York for its commerce, Pennsylvania for its coal, New Jersey for its fruit, and Delaware for the small size of its territory.

*Q.* Name and point out the largest and the smallest of the New-England States.

*Q.* Name and point out the principal cities near the New-Brunswick and Canada boundaries.

*Q.* Name and point out the smallest and the largest of the Middle States.

---

## EXAMINATION LESSON XXIX.

### The Southern and South-Eastern States.

*Q.* Point out on the map, and name, the Southern and South-Eastern States, and their capitals.

*A.* MARYLAND, capital *Annapolis;* VIR-GINIA, capital *Richmond;* KENTUCKY, capital *Frankfort;* TENNESSEE, capital *Nashville;* NORTH CAROLINA, capital *Raleigh;* SOUTH CAROLINA, capital *Columbia;* GEORGIA, capital *Milledgeville;* FLORIDA, capital *Talla-hassee;* ALABAMA, capital *Montgomery;* MIS-SISSIPPI, capital *Jackson;* LOUISIANA, capital *Baton Rouge;* AR-KANSAS, capital *Lit-tle Rock;* and MIS-SOURI, capital *Jef-ferson.*

*Q.* What 9 States lie along the Atlantic coast?

*Q.* What three States lie east of the Mississippi and Ohio rivers?

*Q.* What two States lie west of the Mississippi?

*Q.* Point out and name the capes and bays.

*Q.* What bay cuts Maryland into two parts?

*Q.* What great gulf lies south of Florida?

*Q.* Name and point out the principal rivers.

*Q.* What great river flows into the Gulf of Mexico?

*Q.* What river separates South Carolina from Georgia?

*A.* The Savannah, which rises in the Al-leghany Mountains.

COTTON-PLANT, FLOWER AND POD.

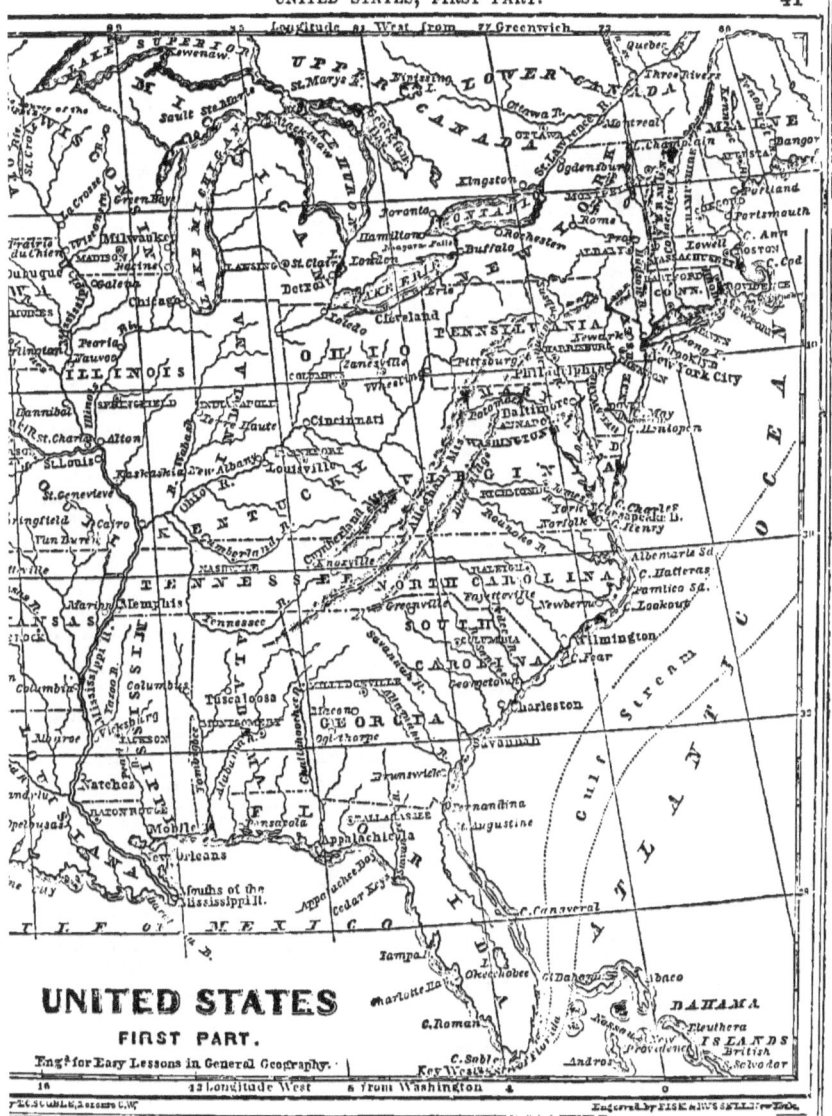

UNITED STATES

FIRST PART.

Engd for Easy Lessons in General Geography.

TOBACCO-PLANT IN FLOWER.

*Q.* What river separates Maryland from Virginia?

*A.* The Potomac; which also rises in the Alleghany Mountains.

*Q.* For what productions are these States noted?

*A.* For their cotton, tobacco, and rice.

*Q.* What chief city is situated in this region?

*A.* Washington, the capital of the Northern United States, in the District of Columbia.

*Q.* Point out and name the capital of each State.

*Q.* Point out the chief cities on the Atlantic coast.

*Q.* Which is the capital of the Southern Confederation?

*A.* Richmond, in the State of Virginia.

---

## EXAMINATION LESSON XXX.

### The Western and South-Western States and Territories.

*Q.* Point out the Western States, and their capitals.

*A.* OHIO, capital *Columbus;* INDIANA, capital *Indianapolis;* MICHIGAN, capital *Lansing;* WISCONSIN, capital *Madison;* ILLINOIS, capital *Springfield;* and MINNESOTA, *St. Pauls.*

*Q.* What three States border on Lakes Erie, Huron, and Superior?

*A.* Ohio, Michigan, and Wisconsin.

*Q.* What States in part border on Lake Michigan?

*A.* Michigan, Indiana, Illinois, and Wisconsin.

*Q.* Which two States lie west of the Mississippi?

*A.* Iowa and Missouri.

*Q.* What three States lie between the Ohio and the Mississippi?

RICE, WITH A GRAIN MAGNIFIED.

*A.* Ohio, Indiana, and Illinois.

*Q.* What four States border on the Mississippi?

*A.* Wisconsin, Iowa, Illinois, and Missouri.

*Q.* For what are these States chiefly noted?

*A.* For their prairies, agriculture, & minerals.

*Q.* Trace the direction of the principal rivers.

*Q.* What chief cities are situated on lakes bordering on Canada?

*Q.* What cities are connected with Canada by railway?

*Q.* Point out and name the South-Western States and Territories, and their capitals.

*A.* TEXAS, capital *Austin;* ARIZONA, capital *Tucson;* NEW MEXICO, capital *Santa Fé;* CALIFORNIA, capital *Sacramento;* NEVADA, capital *Carson;* OREGON, capital *Salem;* WASHINGTON, capital *Olympia;* UTAH, capital *Salt Lake City;* COLORADO, capital *Golden City;* INDIAN TERRITORY, capital *Tahlequah;* KANSAS, capital *Topeka;* NEBRASKA, capital *Omaha;* DAKOTAH, capital *Yankton;* and IOWA, capital *Des Moines.*

*Q.* What States and Territories lie to the east?

*Q.* What States and Territory lie north of Mexico?

*Q.* What States and Territory lie on the Pacific coast?

*Q.* What States and Territories lie south of British America?

*Q.* What States and Territories lie between Missouri and California?

*Q.* Point out the principal capes on the Pacific coast.

*Q.* What great chain of mountains lies between the Mississippi river and the Pacific coast?

*Q.* What great river takes its rise in Dakotah?

*A.* The Missouri, a branch of the Mississippi.

*Q.* What other principal rivers are in these States?

*Q.* What lake is found in Utah?

*A.* Great Salt Lake, near the Mormon city.

*Q.* What river separates Oregon from Washington?

*A.* The Columbia at the north, and the Lewis at the south.

*Q.* What river separates the States of Dakotah, Iowa, and Missouri in part from Nebraska and Kansas?

*A.* The Missouri.

*Q.* What rivers form the eastern and the western boundaries of Texas?

*A.* The Sabine and the Rio Gran-de del Nor-te (or Grand River of the North.)

*Q.* Which are the chief commercial cities in these States?

*A.* San Francisco, in California, and Galveston and Corpus Christi, in Texas.

*Q.* Point out and name the capital or chief city in each State.

# UNITED STATES

## SECOND PART.

Engraved for Easy Lessons in Genl Geogr

## CONVERSATION XVII.

### A Conversational Trip through Mexico.

(See Map of NORTH AMERICA; and Map of the UNITED STATES, Second Part.)

1. Passing down the Gulf of California, we have the peninsular State of Lower California on one side, and the mainland of Mexico on the other.

2. Crossing the isthmus at the boundary of Central America, and rounding the Yucatan peninsula, we enter the Gulf of Mexico. Coasting along it, we reach the Rio Grande del Norte, which is the boundary-river between Mexico and Texas.

---

## EXAMINATION LESSON XXXI.

### The Empire of Mexico.

Q. Trace on the maps named the trip just made.

Q. Point out the position and boundaries of Mexico.

Q. Point out the direction of the great mountain-range.

Q. Point out and name the two peninsulas of Mexico.

A. Lower California, and Yucatan.

Q. Point out and name the chief river at the north.

Q. Point out and name the gulfs and cape.

Q. Point out the position of the capital.

Q. How many states, &c., are included in Mexico?

A. 22 states, 3 territories, and a federal district.

Q. For what is Mexico chiefly noted?

A. For its ancient civilization, its volcanoes, and its silver-mines.

---

## CONVERSATION XVIII.

### Conversational Trip through Central America.

1. Entering Central America from Yucatan, we pass along the coast in an eastern direction until we round Cape Grä-ci-as ä Dios [dee-oce], when we go due south. As the Andes, a continuation of the Rocky Mountains, commence in Central America, we proceed between them, through five separate republics.

## EXAMINATION LESSON XXXII.

### Central America.

Q. Trace on the map the trip just made.

Q. Point out the position of Central America.

Q. What great mountain-ranges extend through it?

A. The Andes of South America.

Q. What countries are included in Central America?

A. 1. Gᴜᴀ-ᴛᴇ-ᴍᴀ-ʟᴀ; 2. Sᴀɴ Sᴀʟ-ᴠᴀ-ᴅᴏʀ; 3. Hᴏɴ-ᴅᴜ-ʀᴀs; 4. Nɪᴄ-ᴀ-ʀᴀ-ɢᴜᴀ [nik-ä-rah-gwä]; 5. Cᴏs-ᴛᴀ Rɪ-ᴄᴀ [ree-kä]; and 6. Bʀɪᴛɪsʜ Hᴏɴ-ᴅᴜ-ʀᴀs.

Q. For what is Central America noted?

A. For being the connecting-link between North and South America, and the dividing-line between the Atlantic and Pacific Oceans.

---

## CONVERSATION XIX.

### Conversational Trip through the West Indies, or West-India Islands.

1. Leaving Cape Gracias a Dios (Central America), on our trip through the West-India Islands, we soon reach the Greater Antilles [an-teels] or Leeward [loo-ard] Islands, and touch at Jamaica, the most important of the British islands. We next visit Cuba. This fine island belongs to Spain; and near Havanna, its capital, Columbus is buried. Crossing Cuba, we see stretching far before us, the Bahama Islands, which belong to Great Britain. It was on one of these islands that Columbus first landed when he discovered the New World. (See map on next page.)

2. Leaving the Bahamas, we touch at Hayti, —part of which (Do-min-ĭ-cä) became a Spanish colony in 1861: the rest is independent. Still going eastward, we reach Porto Rico, another island belonging to Spain.

3. We now sail in a southeasterly direction down by the Caribbean Islands and Lesser Antilles, and touch at a number of small but beautiful islands, belonging to various European powers,—as marked on the map.

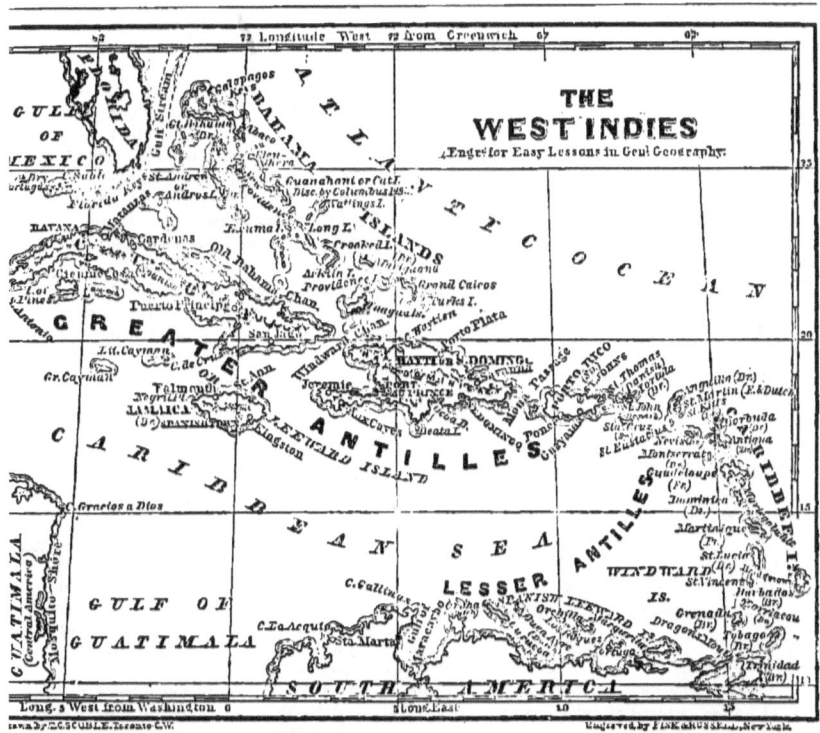

# EXAMINATION LESSON XXXIII.

### The British West-India Islands.

*Q.* Trace on the map the trip just made.

*Q.* Name and point out on the map the British West-india Islands, and their capitals.

*A.* 1. The BAHAMAS, off Florida; capital *Nassau*, on New-Providence Island.

2. JAMAICA, lying south of Cuba; capital *Spanish Town.*

3. The NORTHERN CA-RIB-BEE or LEEWARD ISLANDS, lying east of Porto Rico; capital *St. John.*

4. The WIND-WARD ISLANDS, lying south of the Leeward Islands; capital *Bridgetown*, on Barbados island.

5. TRIN-I-DAD, lying off the coast of South America; capital, *Port of Spain.*

6. The BER-MU-DA ISLANDS, lying 600 miles off North Carolina; capital *Hamilton*, on Long Island.

*Q.* For what are the Bahama Islands chiefly noted?

*A.* For their great number, and for one of them having been the land first reached by Columbus when he discovered the New World.

*Q.* Which are the two largest islands?

*A.* Jamaica and Trinidad.

*Q.* Describe Jamaica.

*A.* Jamaica is 150 miles long and 50 wide. The Blue Mountains traverse its entire length. Turk's Island is attached to Jamaica.

*Q. Name the capital and the chief town of Jamaica.*

*A.* Spanish Town is the capital; but Kingston is the chief place of trade.

*Q. For what is Trinidad chiefly noted?*

*A.* For its size, pitch lakes, and scenery.

*Q. Name its capital.*

*A.* Port of Spain, a very flourishing town.

*Q. What are the chief exports of these islands?*

*A.* Sugar, tobacco, coffee, rice, and fruit.

*Q. Name the principal British Leeward Islands.*

*A.* An-ti-gua [-tee-gä], Do-min-I-cä, St. Christo-pher, Mont-ser-rat, Ne-vis, the Virgin Islands, and Bar-bu-dä.

*Q. Name the principal British Windward Islands.*

*A.* Bar-bä-dos [-doze], St. Vin-cent, To-bä-go, Gren-ä-dä, and St. Lu-ci-ä.

*Q. For what are the Bermuda Islands chiefly noted?*

*A.* For their isolation, coral reefs, and fine climate.

---

## EXAMINATION LESSON XXXIV.

### The Spanish, French, Danish, Swedish, and Dutch West-India Islands.

*Q. Point out and name the Spanish West-India Islands.*

*A.* Cuba, Porto Rico, and part of Hayti.

*Q. Point out and describe the island of Cuba.*

*A.* Cuba is 700 miles long, and is one of the richest and largest of the West-India Islands.

*Q. Name its capital.*

*A.* Havanna, a place of extensive commerce. Near it Columbus is buried.

*Q. Point out and describe the island of Porto Rico.*

*A.* Porto Rico is a beautiful island, and lies east of Hayti. Capital, St. Johns, or San Juan.

*Q. Point out and describe Dominica.*

*A.* Dominica is the eastern part of Hayti, which lies east of Cuba. It is mountainous, but fertile. In 1861 it became a Spanish colony.

*Q. Point out and name the French West-India Islands.*

*A.* Martinique, Gundeloupe, Marie Galante, Desirade, and part of St. Martin.

*Q. Name the principal capitals.*

*A.* St. Pierre is the capital of Martinique; and Basse Terre, of Guadeloupe.

*Q. Point out and name the Danish West-India Islands.*

*A.* Santa Cruz, St. Thomas, and St. John, east of Porto Rico. Capital, Christianstadt.

*Q. Point out and name the Swedish West-India Island.*

*A.* St. Bartholomew, lying between St. Martin and Barbuda : it is the only Swedish colony in America. Capital, Gustavia.

*Q. Point out and name the Dutch West-India Islands.*

*A.* St. Martin (in part), Saba, St. Eustatius, east of Porto Rico ; Buen Ayre, Curaçoa, Oruba, &c., off the coast of South America.

*Q. Which is the most important of the group?*

*A.* Curaçoa. Capital, Williamstadt.

*Q. Are there any other West-India Islands?*

*A.* Yes : Margarita and Tortuga, off the South-American coast; which belong to Venezuela. Capital, Asunçion.

---

## CONVERSATION XX.

### Conversational Trip through South America.

1. Starting from the islands last named, we soon reach the coast of South America. We sail in a southeasterly direction past Venezuela, and British, Dutch, and French Guiana, until we come to the vast empire of Brazil.

2. In sailing along this coast, we pass the mouths of the great river Amazon, and thence to Cape St. Roque. Rounding this cape, we turn to the southward, till we reach Rio de Janeiro, the capital of the empire.

3. Southward from this city, we soon reach Uruguay, La Plata (with its large river of that name), and Patagonia, with the British Falkland Islands to the right, and Tierra del Fuego to the left. Here we round the famous Cape Horn and pass into the Pacific Ocean.

4. We now turn northward, toward Chili, off the coast of which we see the island of Juan Fernandez, the scene of Robinson Crusoe's adventures. We next pass Bolivia, Peru, and Ecuador (or Equador), until we reach New Granada (now Columbia). Crossing the Isthmus of Panama, we once more come to the Caribbean Sea and the West-India Islands.

5. If we now turn our steps inland, and proceed southward along the famous Andes mountains, we pass nearly all the countries of

outh America. At Quito, in Ecuador, we are nder the equator, and here we find the loftest peaks in the entire range of the Andes.

6. In order to reach Paraguay, the only inland country in South America, we enter by the broad mouth of the Rio de la Plata and

go up the Parana and Paraguay rivers. Passing Paraguay, we reach Bolivia and Brazil.

7. If we cross through Bolivia into Peru, we shall come to a source of the Amazon river. Following down this tributary, we reach the great river itself, and pass through Brazil to the Atlantic Ocean. At the mouth of the Amazon we can enter the river Zingu; and ascend its waters, through Brazil, till we come to a tributary of the Paraguay river. Descending it, we again arrive at the mouth of the Rio de la Plata; and so end our journey through South America.

---

## EXAMINATION LESSON XXXV.

### South America.

*Q.* Trace on the map the trip just made.

*Q.* Point out on the map the boundaries of S. America.

*Q.* Name and point out the chief divisions of South America, as follows:

*A.* NEW GRANADA [grä-nah-dä], or CO-LUM-BI-A, capital *Bo-go-ta ;* VEN-EZ-UE-LA [way-lä], capital *Car-a-cas ;* BRITISH GUI-A-NA [ghe-ah-nä], capital *Georgetown ;* FRENCH GUIANA, capital *Cayenne* [kä-yenn]; DUTCH GUIANA, capital *Par-a-mar-i-bo ;* BRA-ZIL', capital *Ri-o de Janeiro* [jä-nee-ro]; ECUA-DOR [ek-wä-dore], capital *Quito* [kee-to]; PE-RU, capital *Lima* [lee-mä]; BO-LIV-I-A, capital *Chuquisaca* [tshu-kĭ-sah-kä]; CHILI [tshil-lī], capital *San-ti-a-go* [-tī-ah-go]; LA PLATA [plah-tä], capital *Purana* [pä-rä-nah]; PARAGUAY [pah'-rä-gway], capital *Asunçion* [ä-soon'-she-own]; URUGUAY [u'-roo-gway], capital *Mon-te Vid-e-o ;* PAT-A-GO-NI-A, TI-ER-RA DEL FU E-GO, and the FA*l*K-LAND ISLANDS.

*Q.* Name and point out the great mountain-range.

*A.* The Andes, running from north to south.

*Q.* Name and point out the great rivers.

*A.* The Amazon and the Rio de la Plata.

*Q.* Point out and name the principal gulfs.

*A.* Venezuela, San Matias, and Penas.

*Q.* Point out and name the principal bays.

*A.* Pin-zon, All Saints, Paranagua [pä-rä-nah-gwä), St. George, Cho-co, and Pan-ä-ma.

*Q.* Point out and name the strait at the south.

*A.* Magellan.

*Q.* Point out and name the principal islands.

*A.* Trinidad, Jo-an-nes, South Georgia, Falkland, Tierra del Fuego, Wellington, Chil-o-e, Juan Fernandez, St. Felix, and Chin-chas.

*Q.* Point out the principal peninsulas.

*A.* Brazil and Patagonia.

*Q.* Point out and name the principal capes.

*A.* Gal-li-nas, Point Ba-ri-ma, Orange, St. Roque, Branco, Frio, St. Maria, Cor-ri-en-tes, Horn, Pillar, St. Nicholas, A-gu-ja, Blanco, St. Lo-ren-zo, St. Francisco, and Point Ma-ri-ald.

---

## EXAMINATION LESSON XXXVI.

### Republics of New Granada or Columbia, and Venezuela.

*Q.* Name and point out on the map the position and boundaries of the republic of New Granada, or Columbia.

*Q.* Point out and name the capes and bays on the coast.

*Q.* What celebrated isthmus of this republic unites North and South America?

*A.* The isthmus of Panama, or Darien.

*Q.* What celebrated range of mountains runs through New Granada, or Columbia?

*A.* The Andes, which are a continuation of the Rocky Mountains of North America.

*Q.* What river flows into the Caribbean Sea?

*A.* The Mag-da-le-na.

*Q.* What other rivers take their rise in New Granada?

*A.* The Orinoco, Rio Negro, and Caqueta.

*Q.* For what is New Granada chiefly noted?

*A.* For its celebrated isthmus of Panama.

*Q.* Name and point out the capital and other chief cities.

*A.* Bogota, the capital; Cartagena, and Panama.

*Q.* Name and point out on the map the position and boundary of Venezuela.

*Q.* Name and point out the cape, gulf, and islands on the coast.

*Q.* Point out the position of Lake Maracaybo.

*Q.* Name and point out the principal rivers.

*A.* The Orinoco and its tributaries.

*Q.* For what is Venezuela chiefly noted?

*A.* For its llanos, or grassy plains.

*Q.* Point out and name the capital.

*A.* Caracas, on the coast.

## EXAMINATION LESSON XXXVII.

### British, French, and Dutch Guiana.

*Q.* Point out the position and boundaries of Guiana.

*Q.* How is it divided?

*A.* Into British, French, and Dutch Guiana.

*Q.* Which division lies to the east, and which to the west?

*A.* The British to the east, and the Dutch to the west.

*Q.* For what is Guiana chiefly noted?

*A.* For its fertility, spices, and dyewoods.

*Q.* What mountain-range separates Guiana from Brazil, and what range from Venezuela?

*A.* The Sierra Acarai from Brazil, and the Pa-ca-rai-na from Venezuela.

*Q.* Point out and name the capitals of each division of Guiana.

*A.* Georgetown, the capital of British, Cayenne, the capital of French, and Paramaribo, the capital of Dutch, Guiana.

## EXAMINATION LESSON XXXVIII.

### The Empire of Brazil.

*Q.* Point out the position and boundaries of Brazil.

*Q.* Point out and name its capes and bays.

*Q.* What countries lie along its northern, western, and southern boundaries?

*A.* Every one in South America except Chili and Patagonia.

*Q.* How many principal mountain-ranges are there?

*A.* Six,—two at the north, one at the south, and three at the east.

*Q.* Point out and name the principal rivers.

*A.* The Amazon and its tributaries; the Araguay and its tributary; and the St. Francisco.

*Q.* Point out and name the principal tributaries of the river Amazon.

*Q.* For what is Brazil chiefly noted?

*A.* For its great rivers, mountains, and forests; its wild animals and birds; and its gold and diamond mines.

*Q.* Point out and name the capital and other chief cities.

*A.* Rio de Janeiro, the capital; Para, Maranham, Pernambuco, Bahia, Victoria, and San Paulo.

## EXAMINATION LESSON XXXIX.

### The Republics of Ecuador and Peru.

*Q.* Point out the position and boundaries of Ecuador.

*Q.* For what is Ecuador chiefly noted?

*A.* For its volcanoes and lofty mountain-peaks.

*Q.* Point out and name its capital.

*A.* Quito, situated near the Equator.

*Q.* Point out the position and boundaries of Peru.

*Q.* Point out and name its capes.

*Q.* What islands lie off the coast?

*A.* The Chinchas or Guano Islands.

*Q.* What river and lake are on its eastern boundary?

*A.* The River Purus and Lake Titicaca.

*Q.* What extent of the Andes is in Peru?

*A.* Nearly one third of that mountain-range.

*Q.* Name the principal rivers in Peru.

*A.* The Ucayali River and its tributaries.

*Q.* For what is Peru chiefly noted?

*A.* For its silver-mines and guano.

*Q.* Name its capital and other chief city.

*A.* Lima, the capital; and Truxillo.

## EXAMINATION LESSON XL.

### The Republics of Bolivia and Chili.

*Q.* Point out the position and boundaries of Bolivia.

*Q.* What mountain and lake are on the N.W. boundary?

*A.* Mount Sorata and Lake Titicaca.

*Q.* For what is Bolivia chiefly noted?

*A.* For its plains, desert sea-coast, and famous silver-mine of Potosi.

*Q.* Point out and name its boundary-rivers.

*A.* The Purus and the Paraguay.

*Q.* Point out and name its capital.

*A.* Chuquisaca, in the interior.

*Q.* Point out the position and boundaries of Chili.

*Q.* For what is it chiefly noted?

*A.* For its narrow width, and extensive coast.

*Q.* What is peculiar about its rivers?

*A.* They all flow into the Pacific Ocean.

*Q.* What islands lie off the coast?

*A.* St. Felix, Chiloe, and Juan Fernandez; the last so famous in connection with the story of "Robinson Crusoe."

*Q.* Name the capital and other chief city.

*A.* Santiago, the capital; and Valparaiso.

## EXAMINATION LESSON XLI.

### La Plata, or the Argentine Republic.

*Q.* Point out the position and boundaries of La Plata.

*Q.* For what is La Plata chiefly noted?

*A.* For its pampas, or vast treeless plains.

*Q.* Name its chief rivers.

*A.* The Parana and the Colorado.

*Q.* What is the direction of these rivers?

*A.* They flow in a south-eastern direction.

*Q.* Name the capital and other chief city.

*A.* Parana, the capital; and Buenos Ayres.

## EXAMINATION LESSON XLII.

### The Republics of Paraguay and Uruguay.

*Q.* Point out the position and boundaries of Paraguay.

*Q.* For what is it chiefly noted?

*A.* For lying entirely inland.

*Q.* Name its two boundary-rivers.

*A.* The Paraguay and the Parana.

*Q.* Point out and name its capital.

*A.* Asunçion, the capital, on the Paraguay.

*Q.* Point out the position and boundaries of Uruguay.

*Q.* For what was it chiefly noted?

*A.* For being the *banda oriental* or southern boundary of Spanish America

*Q.* Name its capital city.

*A.* Montevideo, on the Rio de la Plata.

## EXAMINATION LESSON XLIII.

### Patagonia, Tierra del Fuego, &c.

*Q.* Point out the position and boundaries of Patagonia.

*Q.* What strait separates it from Tierra del Fuego?

*Q.* Point out and name its gulfs, capes, and bay.

*Q.* Name and point out its peninsulas and islands.

*Q.* For what is Patagonia chiefly noted?

*A.* For its sterility and vast plains.

*Q.* For what is Tierra del Fuego noted?

*A.* For its volcanoes. Its name means " Land of Fire."

*Q.* Point out the position of the Falkland Islands.

*Q.* How are they divided?

*A.* Into East Falkland and West Falkland.

*Q.* What other island lies to the south-east?

*A.* South Georgia, an inhospitable place.

## CONVERSATION XXI.

### Conversational Trip through the Continent of Europe.

1. Leaving the shores of America by a Canadian steamer, the first European port we touch at is either a northern or southern one in Ireland. Thence passing within sight of Scotland or of Wales, we soon reach England.

2. We proceed to London, the capital of England and the commercial centre of the world; and from it, by way of Holland and Belgium, direct our steps to England's great neighbour, France. From Paris, by the river Loire [lwahr], we come to the Bay of Biscay, and, passing round Cape Ortegal, coast along, by Portugal and southern Spain, to Gibraltar.

3. Going through this strait, we enter the Mediterranean Sea, and, sailing between the islands of Corsica and Sardinia, reach Italy. Crossing over to the Adriatic Sea and going southward, we coast along Greece, and, passing between Turkey-in-Europe and Turkey-in-Asia, enter the Black Sea.

4. From the mouth of the Danube, we proceed up that noble river through Turkey and Austria, until we come to Germany, with Switzerland on our left. By way of Prussia, we reach the Peninsula of Denmark.

5. Here crossing over through Sweden and Norway, we once more enter the Atlantic Ocean. Coasting northward, we pass the Loffoden Islands, and, rounding North Cape, turn southward through Lapland and Finland, into the vast empire of Russia. We have thus in a rapid tour touched every important country in Europe.

## EXAMINATION LESSON XLIV.

### The Continent of Europe.

*Q.* Trace on the map the trip just made.

*Q.* Point out the position and boundaries of Europe.

*Q.* Point out and name the principal islands.

*A.* The British Isles, Sardinia, Corsica, Sicily.

*Q.* Point out and name some of the smaller islands.

*A.* The islands north of Scotland; the islands east of Spain; Malta, the Ionian Isles, &c.

Q. Point out and name the principal peninsulas.

A. Norway and Sweden, Denmark, Spain and Portugal, Italy, Greece, and the Cri-me-a.

Q. Point out and name the principal capes.

A. North, Clear, Land's End, Ortegal, Finister're, Spartivento, and Mat-a-pan'.

Q. Point out and name the principal seas.

A. White, Baltic, North, Mediterranean, Adriatic, Marmora, Black, Azof, and Caspian.

Q. Point out and name the principal gulfs.

A. Bothnia, Finland, and Cattegat.

Q. Point out and name the principal bay.

A. Biscay, between parts of France and Spain

PRINCIPAL ANIMALS ON THE CONTINENT OF EUROPE.

Q. Point out and name the principal channels.

A. The Irish, St. George's, and the English.

Q. Point out and name the principal straits.

A. Dover, Gibraltar, Messina, and Bosporus.

Q. Point out and name the principal rivers.

A. Volga, Don, Dnieper [nee-per], Dan-ube, hone, E-bro, Ta-gus, Loire, Seine [sehn], hine, Elbe, O-der, and Vis-tu-la.

Q. Point out and name the principal mountains.

A. The Ural or Uralian, Norway or Scandinavian, Valdai Hills, Caucasian, Carpathian, Hartz, Alps, Appenines, and Pyrenees.

Q. Point out and name each of the chief divisions or countries of Europe.

Q. Which of these countries are called first-class powers?

A. Great Britain and Ireland, France, Russia, Austria, and Prussia.

Q. Name the second-class powers.

A. Spain, Italy, Norway and Sweden, Turkey-in-Europe, and the Pontifical States (Rome).

Q. Which are the third-class powers?

A. All the other countries in Europe.

Q. Point out in the above engraving, and name, the principal animals of Europe.

A. 1, The Reindeer; 2, Chamois; 3, Goat; 4, Bull; 5, Cow; 6, Sheep; 7, Horse; 8, Ass; 9, Wild Boar; 10, Owl; 11, Golden Pheasant; 12, Bittern; 13, White Swan.

## EXAMINATION LESSON XLV.

### The British Isles.

Q. oint out the boundaries of the British Isles.

Q. Point out the principal countries in these islands.

A. England and Wales, Scotland, Ireland.

BRITISH ISLES, NORWAY, SWEDEN, DENMARK, AND PART OF GERMANY AND FRANCE, AS SEEN FROM A BALLOON.

BRITISH ISLES.

English Miles.

Eng⁴ for Easy Lessons in Gen¹ Geog?

Q. Point out and name the capitals of England, Ireland, and Scotland.

A. London, Dublin, and Edinburgh.

Q. What islands lie to the west and to the north of Scotland, and to the south of England?

Q. Point out the Channel Islands, Alderney, &c.

Q. What islands lie between England and Ireland?

Q. Point out and name the channels which separate Scotland from Ireland, Wales from Ireland, and southern Wales from southern England.

*Q.* What channel and strait separate England from France?

*Q.* What hills separate England from Scotland?

*Q.* What seas lie to the east and to the west of England?

## EXAMINATION LESSON XLVI.

### The British Empire.

*Q.* What constitutes the British empire?

*A.* The islands of Great Britain and Ireland, and the British Colonies all over the world.

*Q.* What city is the capital of the British empire?

*A.* London, on the river Thames, in England.

*Q.* Who is the chief ruler over the British empire?

*A.* A king or queen. At present, Her Most Gracious Majesty Queen Victoria is chief ruler.

*Q.* How are the British colonies governed?

*A.* By governors (who represent the Queen), aided by various councils of ministers.

## CONVERSATION XXII.

### Conversational Trip through England.

1. From London, the great metropolis, we sail down the Thames, and, rounding southward, proceed through the Strait of Dover, between England and France, to the south coast.

2. In sailing along this coast, we pass the beautiful Isle of Wight and the great naval stations of Portsmouth and Plymouth, till we reach Cornwall,—famous for its tin. Rounding this point, we enter the Bristol Channel, and, crossing it, touch the coast of Wales.

3. Sailing across Cardigan Bay, we come to the Isle of Anglesea, and, passing through the Menai Strait, enter the Irish Sea. Crossing this sea, we touch at the Isle of Man; from which we steer for St. Bees' Head. We now land, and, proceeding through the romantic lake-scenery of Cumberland and Westmoreland, cross over to the North Sea and sail southward to the Norfolk Peninsula. Here we enter the Ouse [oose] river from The Wash, and, going southward, soon reach London, passing the famous university-city of Cambridge.

4. From London we proceed up the Thames

YORK MINSTER

river to Oxford, another great university-city; passing on our left Windsor Castle, one of the Queen's residences. From Oxford we travel northward through the centre of England, passing through a richly-cultivated country, nd many famous manufacturing and mining istricts, where silks, cottons, woollens, iron, nd other articles are manufactured in great bundance. At York, on the river Ouse, we see he celebrated Minster, or Cathedral.

## EXAMINATION LESSON XLVII.

### England.

*Q.* Trace on the map the trip just made.

*Q.* Point out the position and boundaries of England.

*Q.* Point out and name its principal heads and points.

*Q.* Name and point out its principal bays and inlets.

*Q.* Point out and name its principal channels and straits

*Q.* Point out and name its principal islands.

*Q.* Point out and name its principal rivers.

*A.* The Thames [temz], A-von, Sev-ern Mersey, Tyne, Humber, Trent, and Ouse.

Q. Point out the boundaries of Wales.

Q. Point out and name the principal seats of commerce.

A. London, Liverpool, and Bristol.

Q. What are the chief exports?

A. Manufactured cottons, woollens, hardware, and earthenware.

Q. How many counties are there in England?

A. Forty,— 6 northern, 5 eastern, 19 midland, and 10 southern.

Q. How many counties are there in Wales?

A. 12,—6 in North, and 6 in South Wales.

Q. Point out and name the counties in England and Wales.

Q. For what is England chiefly noted?

A. For her civil and religious freedom, and for her commerce and manufactures.

Q. Point out & name her capital & other chief cities.

A. London, the capital; Cambridge, Oxford, Birmingham, Manchester, York, Newcastle, Liverpool, Bristol, Southampton, Portsmouth.

Q. Describe the city of London.

A. London is the largest, wealthiest, and greatest commercial city in the world. Among its most noted public buildings are the Houses of Parliament and the celebrated Westminster Abbey. Population, nearly three millions.

## CONVERSATION XXIII.

### Conversational Trip through Ireland.

1. From Liverpool we take steamer for Ireland, and soon reach its chief city, Dublin. From Dublin, the capital of Ireland and of the province of Leinster, we go southward along the coast, passing in succession the pic-

impressive from its triking grandeur.

3. Passing the counties of Kerry and Clare, we reach Galway, the capital of the province of Connaught. After seeing Erris Head, we round the northern counties of Ireland, passing the celebrated Giant's Causeway, and enter the harbour of Belfast, the capital of the province of Ulster.

4. From Belfast we soon reach Lough Neagh [nay], the largest lake in Ireland; and from it proceed westward across the country to Lough Erne and other beautiful lakes, to the head-waters of the Shannon river. Down this fine river we glide rapidly to its mouth, passing many noted towns on the way. Taking a southerly direction, we are soon in the midst of the mountains of Kerry; among which we find the famous turesque Counties of Wicklow, Wexford, and Waterford, until we come to the city of Cork, capital of the province of Munster and of the largest county in Ireland.

2. After stopping at Queenstown, we still proceed along the coast, and, rounding Cape-Clear Island, turn northward. We now pass in succession deep bays and rocky capes, forming scenery of a most beautiful description, and Lakes of Killarney, where many a day may be spent among the most beautiful scenery of Ireland.

---

## EXAMINATION LESSON XLVIII.

### Ireland.

Q. Trace on the map the trip just made.
Q. Point out the position and boundaries of Ireland.

THE GIANT'S CAUSEWAY, COUNTY ANTRIM.

Q. Point out and name its capes, heads, and points.
Q. Point out and name its chief bays and inlets.
Q. Point out and name the chief rivers.

A. The Shannon, Suir, Barrow, and Boyne.

Q. Point out and name the principal islands.

A. Cape-Clear, Valentia, Arran, Clare, and Achil [ak-il].

Q. Point out and name the principal lakes.

A. Loughs Foyle, Neagh, Erne, Ree, Conn, Mask, Corrib, Derg, and Killarney.

Q. What are the chief exports?

A. Laces, poplins, linens, and farm-products.

Q. Into what provinces is Ireland divided?

A. Leinster, Munster, Ulster, and Connaught.

Q. How many counties are there in Ireland?

A. Thirty-two;—in Leinster, twelve; Munster, six; Ulster, nine; and Connaught, five.

Q. Point out these provinces and counties.

Q. Name the capitals of each of the provinces.

A. Dublin, of Leinster; Cork, of Munster; Belfast, of Ulster; and Galway, of Connaught.

Q. For what is Ireland chiefly noted?

A. For its beautiful scenery, its fertility, and its agricultural or farm products.

Q. Name and point out its chief cities.

A. Dublin, the capital; Belfast, Londonderry, Waterford, Cork, Limerick, Galway.

Q. Describe Dublin, the capital of Ireland.

A. Dublin is one of the finest cities in Europe, and contains a number of elegant public buildings. Population 258,500.

## CONVERSATION XXIV.

### Conversational Trip through Scotland.

1. From Belfast we cross over to Port Patrick, on the west coast of Scotland. Taking a northerly course, we sail past group after group of picturesque islands, including Staffa (with its celebrated cave),—the scenery of which is full of grandeur and beauty.

2. After leaving the Heb-ri-des, or Western Isles, we sail eastward past Cape Wrath and through the Pentland Firth. Turning to the south round the Aberdeen Peninsula, we soon reach the Frith of Forth, on which is situated Edinburgh, the capital of Scotland.

3. From this beautiful city, we cross the country to Glasgow, the chief commercial city of Scotland. Here, on the river Clyde, we see the founderies and shipyards which are so famous for their machinery and ship-building.

4. From Glasgow we pass up Loch Lomond and through Argyle, with the lofty Ben Lomond on our right, to the outlet of the Caledonian Canal, which connects Moray Frith with the Atlantic. Here, leaving Ben Nevis behind, we take a rapid run through the wild scenery of the Northern Highlands.

5. Retracing our steps through Aberdeen by way of Balmoral, on the river Dee, where the Queen's Castle is situated, and crossing the Grampian Mountains, we reach the picturesque counties in the centre of Scotland, with their numerous rivers, lochs, and mountain-peaks, so famous for their beauty. At Loch Katrine in the County of Perth, as at Killarney in Ireland, and at the Cumberland lakes in England, we might linger long; but we must hasten on through the counties of Stirling, Lanark, and Dumfries, and by way of Gretna reach the Solway Frith. Thus we end our trip.

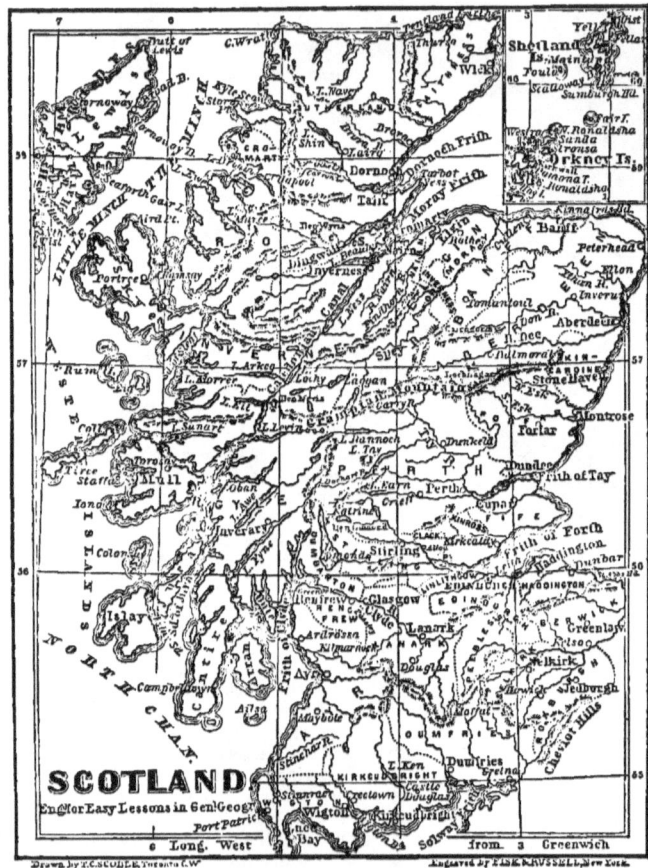

SCOTLAND.

Eng. for Easy Lessons in Gen. Geog.

Drawn by T.C.SCOBLE, Toronto C.W.   Engraved by FISK & RUSSELL, New York.

ri-des, Orkney, and
Shetland Islands.

*Q. Point out and name its principal lochs or lakes.*

*A.* Lochs Lo-
mond, Katrine,
Awe, Fyne, Tay,
Ness, Maree, and
Shin.

*Q. Point out and name its principal mountains.*

*A.* The North
Cheviots, the Gram-
pians, & the North-
ern Highlands.

*Q. Point out and name the principal rivers.*

*A.* The Clyde,
Tay, Dee, and Spey.

*Q. Where is the chief mining-district of Scotland?*

*A.* It stretches
from Fifeshire to
Ayrshire.

*Q. Into how many counties is Scotland divided?*

*A.* 33, includ-
ing the islands.

*Q. Point out on the map, and name, those counties.*

*Q. What are the chief exports?*

*A.* Linens, ma-
chinery, steam-
ships, and agri-
cultural products.

*Q. For what is Scotland chiefly noted?*

*A.* For its moun-
tainous highlands,
wild and picturesque scenery, and many friths.

*Q. Where is Balmoral Castle?*

*A.* On the river Dee, county of Aberdeen.

*Q. Name and point out the principal Scottish cities.*

*A.* Edinburgh, the capital; Glasgow, Dun-
dee, Aberdeen, Perth, St. Andrews, Inverness.

*Q. Describe Edinburgh, the capital of Scotland.*

*A.* Edinburgh is a beautiful and picturesque

## EXAMINATION LESSON XLIX.
—
### Scotland.

*Q.* Trace on the map the trip just made.
*Q.* Point out the position and boundaries of Scotland.
*Q.* Point out and name its capes and heads.
*Q.* Point out its sounds, bays, and firths.
*Q.* Point out and name its principal islands.

*A.* Arran, Islay, Jura, Mull, Skye; the Heb-

BALMORAL CASTLE, THE QUEEN'S HIGHLAND RESIDENCE.

city, and contains many noble buildings and literary institutions. The new town is handsomely laid out. Population 168,100.

## CONVERSATION XXV.

### Conversational Trip through the Principal British Dependencies in Europe.

1. From London we proceed down the English Channel, touching at the islands of Jersey, Guernsey, Alderney, and Sark (or Sereq), which lie close to the coast of France.

2. Leaving these islands, we cross the Bay of Biscay; thence, rounding Spain, touch at the rock of Gibraltar, with its famous fortress. Here entering the Strait of Gibraltar, we pass along the shore of the Mediterranean Sea, and land at Malta, which ends our trip.

## EXAMINATION LESSON L.

### British Dependencies in Europe.

Q. Name the British Dependencies in Europe.
A. The Channel Islands, Gibraltar, Malta, and the Island of Helgoland.

Q. Give the names of the Maltese group of islands.
A. Malta, Gozo, and Cumino.

Q. Give the names of the principal Ionian isles.
A. Corfu, Cephalonia, and Zanté.

Q. Under what government are the Ionian Isles?
A. The Greek; but they formerly were a republic, under the protection of Great Britain.

## CONVERSATION XXVI.

### Conversational Trip through Spain and Portugal.

1. Leaving France by way of the river Rhone, we soon come to Spain; down the coast of which we sail, passing the Isles of Minorca, Majorca, and Iviça on one side, and the mouth of the Ebro river on the other. Round through the Strait of Gibraltar, we reach Portugal, and turn to the north along its coast.

2. On our way northward, we pass two important rivers, the Tagus and the Douro, and again come to the coast of Spain. Rounding Capes Finisterre and Ortegal, we enter the Bay of Biscay. Going due east along the coast, we soon reach the Pyrenees boundary-line between France and Spain.

3. Landing here, we proceed southward to the Strait of Gibraltar, by way of Madrid, the capital of Spain. On our way, we cross successively several mountain-ranges, which divide the country into as many fertile plains and valleys.

## EXAMINATION LESSON LI.

### Spain and Portugal.

Q. Trace on the map of Europe, p. 51, the trip just made.
Q. Point out the boundaries of Spain and Portugal.
Q. Point out and name the capes and strait.
Q. What great mountain-range lies to the north.
Q. For what is Gibraltar noted?
A. For being a celebrated British fortress.

Q. Point out and name the principal rivers.
A. The Ebro, Guadiana, Tagus, and Douro.

Q. What are the chief exports of Spain and Portugal?
A. Wines, oil, fruit, and leather.

Q. Point out and name the capital cities.
A. Madrid, the capital of Spain; and Lisbon, the capital of Portugal.

FRANCE.
IN DEPARTMENTS

2. Here we cross over into the Mediterranean, and proceed along the coast, passing the Rhone river, until we reach Nice, a place lately acquired by France from Sardinia. Going northward along a spur of the Alps, we come to Savoy, also lately ceded to France by Sardinia. Here we reach Mont Blanc; from which we turn to Geneva. Following the Swiss boundary-line to Basle, we go farther N. to Strasbourg.

3. From Strasbourg we proceed by railway across the country to Paris, the capital of France. After seeing this splendid city, we turn our steps southward until we reach the Rhone, down which we go to Avignon; thence to Marseilles, and to Toulon, the southern naval-station of France. From this port we can sail to Corsica, a large island in the Mediterranean belonging to France. Ajaccio, its capital, was the birth-place of the first Napoleon.

*Q.* For what were Spain and Portugal formerly noted?
*A.* For their commercial greatness.

## CONVERSATION XXVII.

### Conversational Trip through France.

1. Our nearest way to France from Russia is through Germany and up the Moselle river. Following the Belgian boundary-line, we reach the Strait of Dover, near Calais. From this town we proceed along the coast, passing Boulogne, Dieppe, Havre (at the mouth of the Seine), Cherbourg, and Brest, until we reach the Bay of Biscay. Down it we sail, passing the rivers Loire and Garonne, until we come to the Pyrenees Mountains, at the south.

## EXAMINATION LESSON LII.

### France.

*Q.* Trace on the map the trip just made.
*Q.* Point out the position and boundaries of France.
*Q.* Point out and name its principal gulf and bay.

*Q.* What mountain-ranges are at the south and the east?
*Q.* Point out the principal rivers, & show their direction.
*Q.* How is France divided?

*A.* Formerly into thirty-four provinces, but now into eighty-six departments.

*Q.* What are the chief exports?

*A.* Silks, fancy articles, and wines.

*Q.* For what is France chiefly noted?

*A.* For its compact shape, its silk-manufactures, and its military power.

*Q.* Point out and name its chief cities.

*A.* Paris, the capital; Calais, Havre, Cherbourg, Brest, Nantes, Bordeaux, Marseilles, Toulon, Lyons, Dijon, Strasbourg, and Rheims.

*Q.* Point out the position of Corsica.
*Q.* Point out and name its capital.

*A.* Ajaccio, the birth-place of Napoleon I.

## CONVERSATION XXVIII.

### Conversational Trip through Austria.

1. From Italy we enter Austria, by way of Venice. Crossing the country we reach the Carpathian Mountains. Following these mountains, we soon come to the river Danube.

2. We now turn to the west, and, following the course of the Danube, pass through the heart of the empire (including Hungary), to Vienna, its capital.

## EXAMINATION LESSON LIII.

### The Empire of Austria.

*Q.* Trace on the map of Europe, p. 51, the trip just made.
*Q.* Point out the position and boundaries of Austria.
*Q.* Point out and name its principal mountain-ranges?

*A.* The Alps and the Carpathians.

*Q.* Point out and name its principal river.

*A.* The Danube, flowing through its centre.

*Q.* Point out and name the principal divisions of Austria.

*A.* Austria Proper, Venice, and Hungary.

*Q.* What are the chief exports?

*A.* Glass, flax, paper, silk, and wool.

*Q.* For what is Austria noted?

*A.* For its central position and its mines.

*Q.* Point out and name some of its chief cities.

*A.* Vienna, the capital; Innspruck, and Venice.

## CONVERSATION XXIX

### Conversational Trip through Prussia.

1. From Austria we cross the Hartz Mountains into Prussia by way of Saxony. Journeying to the north-east through Silesia and across the rivers Oder and Vistula, we reach the Baltic.

2. Turning now to the west and passing the mouth of the Oder, we proceed inland to Berlin, the capital of Prussia; then turning to the west, we cross the Elbe through Hanover into Eastern Prussia, travelling through a fertile country.

## EXAMINATION LESSON LIV.

### Prussia.

*Q.* Trace on the map of Europe, p. 51, the trip just made.
*Q.* Point out the position and boundaries of Prussia.
*Q.* What countries separate East and West Prussia?

*A.* Hanover, and other smaller states.

*Q.* Point out and name the principal rivers.

*A.* The Rhine, Elbe, Oder, and Vistula.

*Q.* In what direction do they flow?
*Q.* What are the chief exports of Prussia?

*A.* Grain, wine, lumber, wool, and linen.

*Q.* For what is Prussia chiefly noted?

*A.* For its rapid growth into a kingdom.

*Q.* Point out and name its capital city.

*A.* Berlin, on a tributary of the Elbe.

## CONVERSATION XXX.

### Conversational Trip through Italy.

1. Leaving Switzerland, we pass through Piedmont to Turin, its capital, and, by railway, reach the Gulf of Genoa. Going down the coast of Tuscany, we sail between the islands of Elba and Corsica.

2. Leaving the island of Sardinia to the west, we pass in succession the river Tiber and the beautiful Bay of Naples, till we reach the Strait of Messina, between Italy and the island of Sicily. On leaving the strait, we round Cape Spartivento, and, passing the Gulfs of Squil-la-ce and Taranto, enter, by the Strait of Otranto, the Adriatic Sea.

3. Up this sea we sail rapidly until we reach the Gulf of Trieste. Crossing this gulf to

Venice, we go southward to the river Po, and ascend its rich valley for some distance, then turn southward through Parma, Modena, and Tuscany. From the celebrated city of Rome, we can proceed to the south of Italy, by way of the Apennine Mountains, which extend as far as the Strait of Messina.

## EXAMINATION LESSON LV.

### The Italian States.

*Q.* Trace on the map the trip just made.

*Q.* Point out the position and boundaries of Italy.

*Q.* Point out and name the principal capes and straits.

*Q.* Point out and name its principal gulfs and bays.

*Q.* What large islands lie off its coast?

*A.* Corsica, Sardinia, and Sicily.

*Q.* Point out and name its principal mountain-ranges.

*A.* The Alps and the Apennines.

*Q.* Point out and name its principal rivers.

*A.* The Po, Arno, and Tiber.

*Q.* In what direction do they flow?

*Q.* Name its two celebrated volcanic mountains.

*A.* Vesuvius, at Naples; and Etna, in Sicily.

*Q.* How is Italy divided?

*A.* Into the kingdom of Italy, the Austrian province of Venetia, and the Pontifical States.

*Q.* What are the chief exports?

*A.* Silks, olives, straw-hats, and coral.

*Q.* For what is Italy chiefly noted?

*A.* For its ancient greatness; and for having long been the residence of the Pope, or head of the Roman-Catholic Church.

*Q.* Point out and name its chief cities?

*A.* Turin, Genoa, Milan, Venice, Bologna, Florence, Pisa, Rome, Naples, and Palermo.

*Q.* For what is Rome noted?

*A.* Rome, the capital of the Pontifical States, is noted for its numerous splendid buildings, especially the Pontifical Cathedral of St. Peter, the Vatican (or residence of the Pope), and numerous churches. Pop. 180,500.

## CONVERSATION XXXI.

### Conversational Trip through Switzerland.

1. From Spain we reach Switzerland through France, by way of Mont Blanc and the Great St. Bernard (see map of Italy). Turning to the east along the southern boundary between Switzerland and Italy (see map of Europe), we are in the midst of numerous lakes, and of some of the most celebrated scenery of the Alps.

2. Going northward, we reach Berne, the capital of Switzerland, and then, turning southward, come to the Lake of Geneva, at the south-west corner of Switzerland (see map of France). From this beautiful lake, we soon again reach the celebrated Mont Blanc and the Great St. Bernard; and so end our trip.

## EXAMINATION LESSON LVI.

### Switzerland.

*Q.* Trace on the map of Europe (p. 51), and map of Italy (page 63, opposite), the trip just made.

*Q.* Point out the position and boundaries of Switzerland.

*Q.* What mountains form its southern boundary?

*A.* The Alps, which separate it from Italy.

*Q.* Name two mountain-peaks near this boundary.

*A.* Mont Blanc and the Great St. Bernard.

*Q.* Name one of the principal lakes.

*A.* Geneva, on the French boundary-line.

*Q.* What are the chief exports?

*A.* Jewelry, ribbons, silks, cattle, and cheese.

*Q.* For what is Switzerland chiefly noted?

*A.* For its beautiful lakes and mountains.

*Q.* How is Switzerland divided?

*A.* Into 22 cantons, forming a republic.

*Q.* Point out and name the chief cities.

*A.* Berne, the capital; and Geneva.

## CONVERSATION XXXII.

### Conversational Trip through Russia-in-Europe.

1. From Stockholm, opposite the Gulf of Finland, we sail eastward to St. Petersburg, the capital of Russia. After seeing this fine place, we proceed inland to Moscow, the former capital. Here we find a splendid city; but as we pass out of it toward the Dnieper river, we enter a desolate country, called the Steppes.

2. From the mouth of the Dnieper we reach the Crimea, and, after visiting Sebastopol and

its famous battle-ground, proceed along the Black Sea to the Sea of Azof. Here we enter the river Don for a short distance, and, crossing over from it to the Caspian Sea by way of the river Volga, turn northward till we come to the mouth of the Ural river.

3. Up this river we go some distance, then cross to the Ural Mountains and sail down the Petchora river to the Arctic Ocean. We now turn to the west and enter the White Sea; down which we proceed, and, crossing by river to Lake Onega, are soon at St. Petersburg again.

*Q.* What are the chief exports?

*A.* Tallow, hides, iron, hemp, furs, and timber.

*Q.* For what is Russia chiefly noted?

*A.* For its great extent, and its steppes.

*Q.* Name and point out its principal cities.

*A.* St. Petersburg, the capital; Moscow, the former capital; and Sebastopol.

*Q.* Point out the position of Poland.

*A.* It lies between Russia and Prussia.

*Q.* Point out and name its chief town.

*A.* Warsaw, the former capital, on the river Vistula.

## CONVERSATION XXXIII.

### Conversational Trip through Norway and Sweden.

1. From London we sail northeastwardly to the coast of Norway. Up this coast we proceed, passing a great number of fiords, or bays, on the coast, until we reach the Loffoden Isles and North Cape.

2. After rounding the peninsula and crossing Lapland, we enter the Gulf of Bothnia. We sail down this gulf to Stockholm, the capital of the kingdom. We now continue our course in the Baltic Sea, and, rounding the Swedish peninsula, soon enter the Cattegat.

3. Passing up the Cattegat, we reach Christiania, the capital of Norway; and leaving it on a trip northward through Norway, travel amidst wild and mountainous scenery.

## EXAMINATION LESSON LVII.

### Russia-in-Europe.

*Q.* Trace on the map of Europe, p. 51, the trip just made.

*Q.* Point out on the same map the position and boundaries of Russia-in-Europe.

*Q.* Point out and name its principal seas and gulfs.

*Q.* Point out its principal capes and peninsulas.

*Q.* Point out and name its principal mountain-ranges.

*A.* The Ural and the Caucasian Mountains.

*Q.* Point out and name its principal rivers.

*A.* The Pet-cho-ra, Dwi-na, Du-na, Vis-tu-la in part, Dnieper, Don, Volga, and U-ral.

## EXAMINATION LESSON LVIII.

### Norway and Sweden.

*Q.* Trace on the map the trip just made.

*Q.* Point out the boundaries of Norway and Sweden.

*Q.* Point out and name their principal capes, gulfs, &c.

*Q.* What chiefly divides these two countries?

*A.* An extensive mountain-range.

*Q.* Point out and name the principal lakes.

*A.* Mu-lar, Wen-er, and Wetter.

*Q.* Point out and name the principal rivers.

*A.* Muonio, Tornea, Dahl, Go-tha, and Glommen.

*Q.* What are the chief exports?

*A.* Iron, copper, fish, and horses.

*Q.* Name the capital of each country.

*A.* Stockholm, the capital of Sweden; and Christiania, the capital of Norway.

*Q.* Where is Lapland, and to whom does it belong?

*A.* It lies to the north-east of Sweden, and belongs partly to Sweden and partly to Russia.

## CONVERSATION XXXIV.

### Conversational Trip through Denmark.

Leaving Prussia by the river Elbe, we reach Denmark. Sailing northward along the coast, we pass many islands, and enter the Cattegat. Rounding this, we move southward, and soon enter the Elbe again.

## EXAMINATION LESSON LIX.

### Denmark.

*Q.* Point out the position and boundaries of Denmark.

*Q.* Name the principal islands off its east coast.

*A.* Zealand, Funen, and Laaland.

*Q.* What are the chief exports?

*A.* Fish, agricultural products, and feathers.

*Q.* For what is Denmark chiefly noted?

*A.* For its peninsular form.

*Q.* Point out and name its chief cities.

*A.* Copenhagen, the capital; and Elsinore.

## CONVERSATION XXXV.

### Conversational Trip through Holland and Belgium.

1. From Denmark we reach Holland, either through Hanover or by the North Sea. Sailing along the low flat coast, we pass numerous islands until we come to the mouth of the Rhine. Passing this wide river-delta, we reach Belgium.

2. Landing at the boundary-line between France and Belgium, we follow it into Holland until we come to the Rhine again. Crossing the Rhine, we still continue northward until we arrive at Amsterdam, the capital of Holland.

## EXAMINATION LESSON LX.

### The Kingdoms of Holland and Belgium.

*Q.* Point out the boundaries of Holland and Belgium.

*Q.* What principal river has its outlet on the coast?

*A.* The Rhine, which rises in Germany.

*Q.* What are the chief exports?

*A.* Cheese, gin, tulips, lace, linen, and clocks.

*Q.* For what is Holland chiefly noted?

*A.* For its numerous canals, and for its dykes or coast-embankments to keep out the sea.

*Q.* For what is Belgium chiefly noted?

*A.* For its oil-paintings; and for having been one of the principal battle-fields of Europe.

*Q.* Point out and name the capital cities.

*A.* Amsterdam, the capital of Holland; and Brussels, the capital of Belgium.

## CONVERSATION XXXVI.

### Conversational Trip through Germany Proper.

We have already gone through Austria, Prussia, Denmark, and Holland,—parts of all of which are included in the Germanic Confederation. Following the course of the Elbe, we pass through Saxony and several other small kingdoms, duchies, grand duchies, &c., known as Germany Proper, and which are also included in the Confederation.

## EXAMINATION LESSON LXI.

### The Germanic Confederation.

*Q.* Point out and name the several countries in the Germanic Confederation.

*A.* Parts of Austria, Prussia, Denmark, and Holland; and Germany Proper, including the kingdoms of Hanover, Saxony, Bavaria, and Wurtemberg; and 27 smaller states.

*Q.* For what object are these states confederated?
*A.* Chiefly for commerce and self-defence.

*Q.* Point out & name the chief rivers in these countries.
*A.* The Oder, Elbe, Rhine, and Danube.

*Q.* What are the chief exports?
*A.* Flax, grain, timber, and fruit.

*Q.* Name the capital cities of some of these States.
*A.* Hanover, the capital of Hanover; Dresden, of Saxony; Munich, of Bavaria; Stutgard, of Wurtemberg.

## CONVERSATION XXXVII.

### a versational Trip through Turkey-in-Europe and Greece.

1. To reach Turkey from Holland, we go up the Rhine until we can cross over to the Danube. Sailing down this noble river through Austria, and Turkey - in - Europe, we soon come to its mouth, on the Baltic Sea. From this point we proceed southward as far as the Bosporus, and passing Constantinople, the capital of Turkey, go through the Sea of Marmora into the Grecian Archipelago.

2. Sailing through this archipelago, we soon reach the classic shores of Greece, and Athens, its capital. From Athens we go southward, and, rounding Cape Matapan', sail northward to the Ionian Islands. Passing them, we again come to the Turkish coast. Following this coast up the Adriatic, we once more arrive at the Austrian boundary. From this point we can easily cross the country to the river Danube again.

## EXAMINATION LESSON LXII.

### The Kingdom of Greece.

*Q.* Trace on the map of Europe, p. 51, the trip just made.
*Q.* Point out the position and boundaries of Greece.
*Q.* Point out and name its principal cape.
*Q.* How is Greece divided?
*A.* Into Hellas, at the north; and the Morea, a peninsula, at the south.

*Q.* Point out the principal islands off the coast.
*A.* Candia, belonging to Turkey; and the Ionian Islands, annexed to Greece.

*Q.* What are the chief exports?
*A.* Honey; currants, figs, and other fruits.

*Q.* For what is Greece chiefly noted?
*A.* For its ancient greatness.

*Q.* Point out and name its capital city.
*A.* Athens, on its eastern coast.

## EXAMINATION LESSON LXIII.

### Turkey-in-Europe.

*Q.* Point out the boundaries of Turkey-in-Europe.
*Q.* Point out and name its principal mountains.
*A.* The Carpathians, at the north.

*Q.* Point out and name its principal river.
*A.* The Danube, at the north.

*Q.* What are the chief exports?
*A.* Carpets, silks, leather, drugs, and fruit.

*Q.* For what is Turkey-in-Europe chiefly noted?
*A.* For its ancient history as Macedonia.

*Q.* Point out and name the capital city of the empire.
*A.* Constantinople, on the Bosporus.

## EXAMINATION LESSON LXIV.

### The Continent of Asia.

*Q.* Point out the position and boundaries of Asia.
*Q.* Point out and name its principal capes and bays.
*Q.* Point out and name its principal seas and gulfs.
*Q.* Point out and name its chief peninsulas.
*A.* Turkey-in-Asia, Arabia, Hindostan', Malacca, Corea, and Kamtchatka.

*Q.* Point out and name the principal islands.
*A.* Ceylon', Hainan', Formosa, the Japan Isles, Saghali'en, and New Siberia.

*Q.* Point out and name the principal mountain-ranges.
*A.* The Yablonoi, Altai, Thian-shan', Peling', the Eastern and Western Ghauts, Himalay'as, and the Ural and the Caucasus in part.

*Q.* Point out and name the great rivers in Asia.
*A.* Indus, Ganges, Mekong', Yang-tse-ki-ang', Ho-ang-ho', Amoor', Lena, Yenisei, and Obi.

*Q.* Point out and name the principal desert.
*A.* The great desert of Gobi, in Tartary.

*Q.* Into what countries is Asia divided?
*A.* Into Russia - in - Asia, Turkey - in - Asia, Arabia, Persia, Independent Tartary, Bokhara,

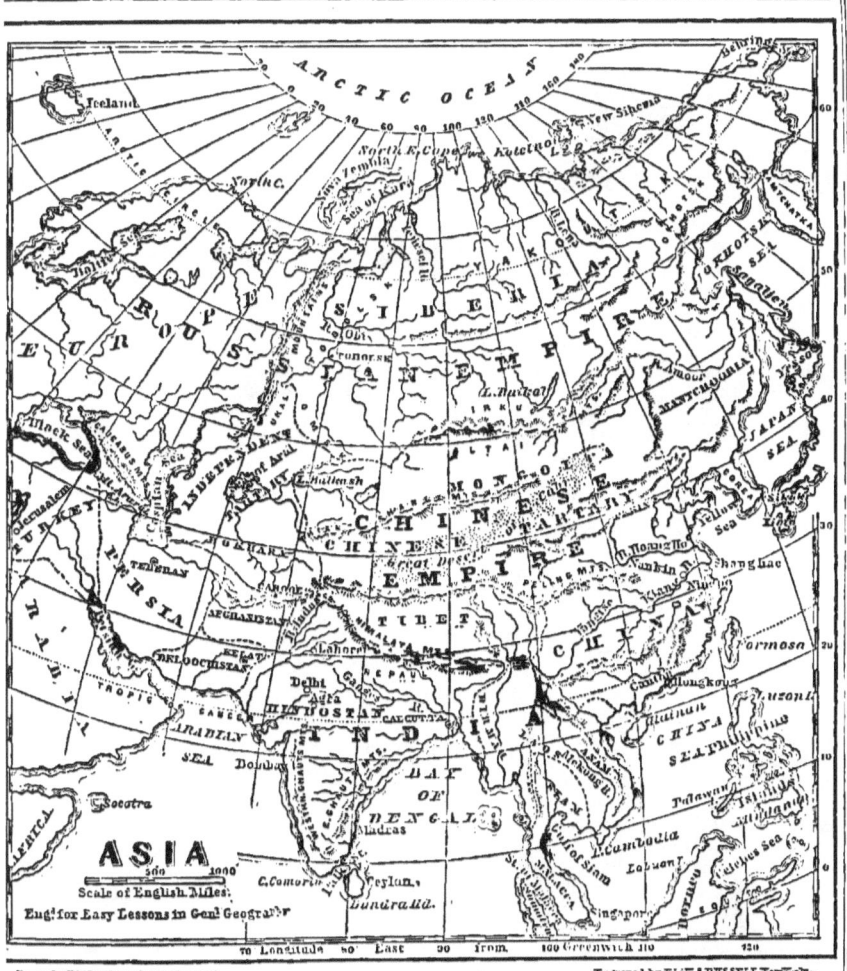

Afghanistan', Beloochistan', Hindostan', Burmah (or Birmah), Siam, Laos, An'am, Malacca, China, Japan, &c.

*Q.* What countries lie east of Persia?—east of Hindostan?—north of India?—east of the Caspian Sea? What islands lie to the east?—to the north?—to the south? What range of very high mountains lies north of Hindostan?

PRINCIPAL ANIMALS ON THE CONTINENT OF ASIA.

## CONVERSATION XXXVIII.

### Conversational Trip through Asia.

1. From Turkey-in-Europe we cross over to Turkey-in-Asia, and, on our way to Arabia, pass through Jerusalem, the capital of Palestine, now called Syria. From Arabia we cross over to Persia, and through Afghanistan and Beloochistan reach India. Here, sailing down the Ganges river, we enter the Bay of Bengal.

2. Following the coast-line to the Malacca or Malay Peninsula, we enter the Gulf of Siam, and, turning northward, soon come to China. Passing along this extensive coast, we touch at the Corea on our way through the Japan Islands. From Japan we continue our course, by way of Kamtchatka, to Behring Strait.

3. Here we reach the Arctic Ocean; and, following the coast-line past Siberia, we enter the mouth of the river Lena. Sailing up this river to its western source, we continue on through Lake Baikal to the foot of the Altai Mountains. Crossing these mountains into Mongolia, Chinese Tartary, and Tibet, we come to the Himalaya Mountains.

4. If we wish to explore China, we can now turn to the east, and, reaching the Yang-tse-kiang river, proceed eastward through the heart of that great empire.

5. But continuing our course along the foot of the Himalaya Mountains, by way of Cabool, we enter a small river. Down this river we sail to the Sea of Aral; and from it, across Independent Tartary, reach the Caspian Sea. Sailing down this sea, we come to a river on its west coast. Up this river we proceed to Mount Ararat; from which we again reach Turkey-in-Asia, and thus end our trip.

Q. Trace on the map of Asia the trip just made.

Q. Point out and name the principal animals of Asia.

A. 1, The Monkey; 2, Lion; 3, Tiger; 4, Ibex; 5, Camel; 6, Elephant; 7, Rhinoceros; 8, Peacock; 9, Flamingo; 10, Boa-Constrictor; and 11, Anaconda.

## CONVERSATION XXXIX.

### Conversational Trip through Russia-in-Asia.

1. From the Black Sea we journey to the Caspian Sea. From this sea, we reach the boun-

proceeding up it, pass
s into Siberia. Cross-
ue to the Yenisei river,
ich the Arctic Ocean.
north-cast, we round
touching at the islands
ue our course through
iy of Kamtchatka, to
ifter passing Saghalicn
ird to the river Amoor.
ry-river, we reach the
continuing our course
iome to the Obi river.

## LESSON LXV.

.n-Asia.

iia the trip just made.
as of Russia-in-Asia.
if Siberia.
principal mountain-range.
it the south.
rivers, and their courses.
Lena, and Amoor.
orts?
ucts of the mines.
sia chiefly noted?
l Siberian penal-mines.
y of Siberia.
ich of the river Obi.

## TION XL.

through Turkey-
iia.

a, we cross over to the
ious in Bible history;
continue our course to
ar which is supposed
of Eden.
we go as far as the
g our steps, we proceed
iundary-line between
r Mount Ararat, and
ck Sea.

## EXAMINATION LESSON LXVI.

### Turkey-in-Asia.

*Q.* Trace on the map of Asia the trip just made.

*Q.* Point out the position of Turkey-in-Asia.

*Q.* Name the principal divisions of Turkey-in-Asia.

*A.* Asia Minor, comprising Syria (including Palestine), Armenia, Kourdistan' (or Assyria).

*Q.* What are the chief exports?

*A.* Fruit, grain, coffee, and silk.

*Q.* For what is Turkey-in-Asia chiefly noted?

*A.* For having been the place where nearly all the events mentioned in Scripture occurred.

*Q.* For what is Palestine chiefly noted?

*A.* For having been the scene of OUR SA-VIOUR'S life and sufferings on earth.

## CONVERSATION XLI.

### Conversational Trip through Arabia, Persia, Afghanistan, and Beloochistan.

1. From Jerusalem, we go southward to Arabia, and thence continue our course down the coast. Turning to the cast, and keeping along the coast, we enter the Persian Gulf.

2. At the head of this gulf, we turn southward along the Persian coast, and soon come to the western boundary of India. Turning inland to the north, we cross Beloochistan, by way of Kel-at', into Afghanistan. Still continuing northward, we reach Cab-ool'. From Cabool we cross the mountains into Persia.

3. Here, through a great salt-desert, we proceed to the Caspian Sea; and from it turn southward to Teheran', the capital of Persia. From Teheran we proceed directly southward, through a mountainous country, to the head of the Persian Gulf, as before.

## EXAMINATION LESSON LXVII.

### Arabia.

*Q.* Trace on the map of Asia the trip just made.

*Q.* Point out the position of Arabia.

*Q.* What gulf separates Arabia from Persia?

*Q.* What is peculiar about Arabia?

*A.* Though a large country, its rivers are small, as mountains extend all round the coast.

*Q.* What are the chief exports?

*A.* Coffee, gums, spices, and fruits.

*Q.* For what is Arabia chiefly noted?

*A.* For its sandy deserts, and for having been the scene of the impostor Mahomet's career.

*Q.* Name the capital city.

*A.* Mecca, inland from its west coast.

---

## EXAMINATION LESSON LXVIII.

### Persia, Beloochistan, and Afghanistan.

*Q.* Point out the position and boundaries of Persia.

*Q.* What seas lie N. of Persia, and S. of Beloochistan?

*A.* The Caspian, north of Persia; and the Arabian, south of Beloochistan.

*Q.* What gulf lies south of Persia?

*Q.* What are the chief exports?

*A.* Silks, carpets, and perfumes.

*Q.* What are these countries noted for?

*A.* Persia is noted for its ancient greatness, and the other states for their warlike tribes.

*Q.* Point out and name the capital cities.

*A.* Teheran, the capital of Persia; Cabool, the capital of Afghanistan; and Kelat, the capital of Beloochistan.

---

## CONVERSATION XLII.

### Conversational Trip through the East Indies.

1. From Beloochistan we proceed by the Arabian Sea along the coast-line of India, and pass in succession the mouths of the Indus river, the Gulfs of Cutch and Cambay, the city of Bombay', and Goa the capital of the Portuguese settlements. To the west of the Malabar coast lie the Laccadive and the Maldive Islands.

2. Rounding Cape Comorin, we pass the island of Ceylon' to the right, and proceed up the Bay of Bengal' to Pondicherry the capital of the French settlements, Madras' the capital of the Madras Presidency, and the mouths

of the Kistnah, Godavery, and Hoogly rivers, until we reach the river-delta of the Ganges.

3. From the mouths of the Ganges and the Bramahpootra rivers we turn to the south along the coast-line of Arracan', where, rounding the peninsula of Pegu, we pass the mouth of the Irrawaddy and come to the Tenasserim coast; down which we sail to Singapore, the capital of the British settlements on the Malacca Straits. (See map of Asia.)

4. Crossing the Bay of Bengal, we reach the Hoogly river; up which we go to Calcutta, the capital of the Bengal Presidency and of British India. From Calcutta we proceed northward to the river Ganges. Sailing up this noble river, with the great Himalaya Mountains to the north of us, we come to the Agra Presidency, and pass through many splendid cities. Continuing our course to the north-west after we leave the Ganges, we reach the Punjaub' Presidency, which is enclosed within five rivers. Crossing four of them, which are tributaries of the Indus river, we turn southward down this fine river, and again enter its many mouths.

---

## EXAMINATION LESSON LXIX.

### Hindostan, or British India.

*Q.* Trace on the map of India the trip just made.

*Q.* Point out the boundaries of British India.

*Q.* Point out and name its principal capes, gulfs, & bays.

*Q.* Point out and name its principal islands.

*A.* Ceylon, the Maldives, and the Laccadives.

*Q.* Point out and name its principal mountains.

*A.* The Himalayas, at the north; and the Ghauts, at the south.

*Q.* Point out the principal rivers, and their courses.

*A.* The Indus, Ganges, Bramahpootra, Godavery, Kistnah, and Nerbudda.

*Q.* What are the chief exports?

*A.* Rice, sugar, tea, spices, indigo, cotton, opium, silk, hemp, flax, iron, and salt.

*Q.* For what is India chiefly noted?

*A.* For being the largest and most valuable dependency of the British crown.

*Q.* How is Hindostan divided?

*A.* Into the five British Presidencies, &c.; and the dependent and the independent states.

*Q.* Point out and name the principal divisions.

*A.* The eastern British provinces (of Burmah, or Birmah); the empire of Burmah, the kingdom of Siam, the empire of Anam, and the Laos Country.

*Q.* What does British Burmah include?

*A.* Assam, Arracan, Pegu, and Tenasserim, on the east coast of the Bay of Bengal.

*Q.* Point ont and name its principal rivers.

*A.* The Irrawaddy and the Mekong'.

*Q.* Point out the British Presidencies and capitals.

*A.* Bengal', *capital* Calcutta; Agra, *capital* Agra; Punjaub', *capital* Lahore'; Bombay' and Madras', *capitals* Bombay and Madras.

*Q.* Point out and name other chief cities of India.

*A.* Delhi, Lucknow, Patna, Surat', Hyderabad'; and Colombo, in Ceylon.

*Q.* Point out the principal independent or non-British states of Hindostan.

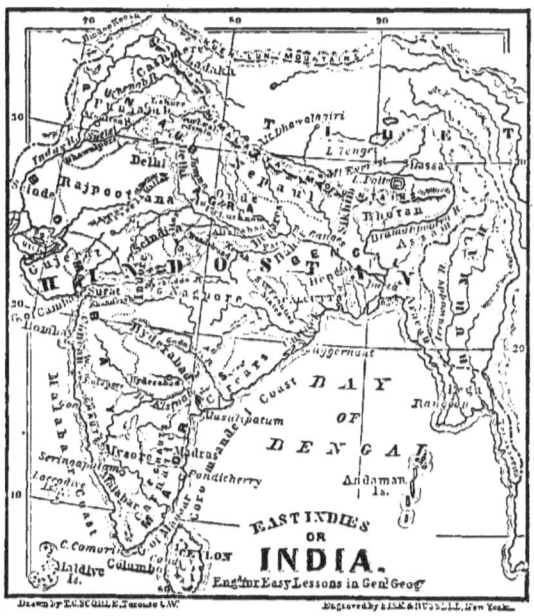

EAST INDIES OR INDIA.

Eng'dfor Easy Lessons in Gen'l Geog'y

*A.* Pondicherry (French) and Goa (Dutch) settlements; and Cashmere', Nepaul', and Bhotun', native states.

---

EXAMINATION LESSON LXX.

Burmah, Siam, &c.

*Q.* Point out the boundaries of Burmah and Siam.
*Q.* Point ont and name the capital cities.

*A.* Singapore', capital of the British Malacca-Straits settlements; Monchobo, of Burmah; Bankok', of Siam; Hue, of Anam.

---

CONVERSATION XLIII.

Conversational Trip through the Chinese Empire.

1. From Anam (see map of Asia), we sail along the Chinese coast, passing the large islands of Hainan' and Formosa, and the coast-cities of Canton', Ningpo,' and Shanghae', until we reach the mouth of the Yang-tse-ki-ang river. Up this great river we proceed to Nankin', and then on through the heart of the empire until we come to Tibet and the desert of Gobi.

2. Crossing this desert to the Thian-Shan' Mountains, we proceed along them to the east; and again cross the desert of Gobi to Pekin', the capital of the empire. After seeing this great city, we continue our course from it into the Yellow Sea, and thence to the mouth of the Ho-ang-ho river. On our way, we may meet with many groups of people like that in the engraving on next page.

---

EXAMINATION LESSON LXXI.

The Empire of China.

*Q.* Trace on the map of Asia the trip just made.
*Q.* Point out the position and boundaries of China.

CHINESE MANDARIN, HIS WIFE, CHILD, AND SERVANT.

Q. Point out and name its principal seas.

Q. Point out and name its principal mountains.

A. The Thian-shan, north, and the Peling, south of Chinese Tartary.

Q. Point out and name the principal rivers.

A. The Ho-ang-ho and the Yang tse-ki-ang.

Q. How is China divided?

A. Into China Proper, Tibet, Chinese Tartary (including Mongolia, and Mantchooria), Corea; and Formosa, Hainan, and Loo-choo islands.

Q. What are the chief exports?

A. Tea, rice, silks, porcelain, and nankeen.

Q. For what is China chiefly noted?

A. For its vast population, its great wall, its tea-exports, and its porcelain or china.

Q. Point out and name its chief cities.

A. Pekin, the capital; Nankin, Shanghae, Ningpo, and Canton.

Q. Point out and name the British possessions in China.

A. The island of Hong-Kong' (capital Victoria); and Cowloon', opposite Hong-Kong.

Q. What other Europeans have Chinese possessions?

A. The Portuguese have Macao.

## CONVERSATION XLIV.

### Conversational Trip through the Islands of Japan.

From China we cross over to Ximo (or Kiusiu), Sikokf, Niphon, and Yesso, the principal islands of Japan. As we wind in and out through the straits and deep gulfs and bays, we see many places of great beauty, and cities well populated. To the north are Saghali'en and the Kurile islands, which belong to Japan.

## EXAMINATION LESSON LXXII.

### The Islands of Japan.

Q. Point out the position of the Japan islands.

Q. Name the principal islands of Japan.

A. Ximo (or Kiusiu), Sikokf, and Niphon. Yesso, the southern part of Saghalien, and the Kurile islands, are dependencies.

Q. What are the chief products?

A. Copper, iron, tea, tobacco, and silk.

Q. For what is Japan chiefly noted?

A. For its long seclusion from other nations.

Q. Point out and name its chief cities.

A. Jeddo, the military capital; Meaco, the ecclesiastical capital; Osaka, and Simoda.

## EXAMINATION LESSON LXXIII.

### Oceania.

Q. Point out the great island-groups of Oceania.

Q. Into how many great groups are they divided?

A. Into three, called Malaysia, Australasia, and Polynesia; and these are again subdivided.

## EXAMINATION LESSON LXXIV.

### Malaysia.

Q. Point out the position of the Malaysian group.

Q. Name the principal islands in this group.

A. Java, Borneo, Celebes, and the Philippines.

Q. Name the principal Dutch islands in Malaysia.

A. Java, Cel-e-bes, part of Borneo, and Ti-mor.

Q. Name the Spanish islands in Malaysia.

A. The Philippines, a group of three large and twelve hundred smaller islands.

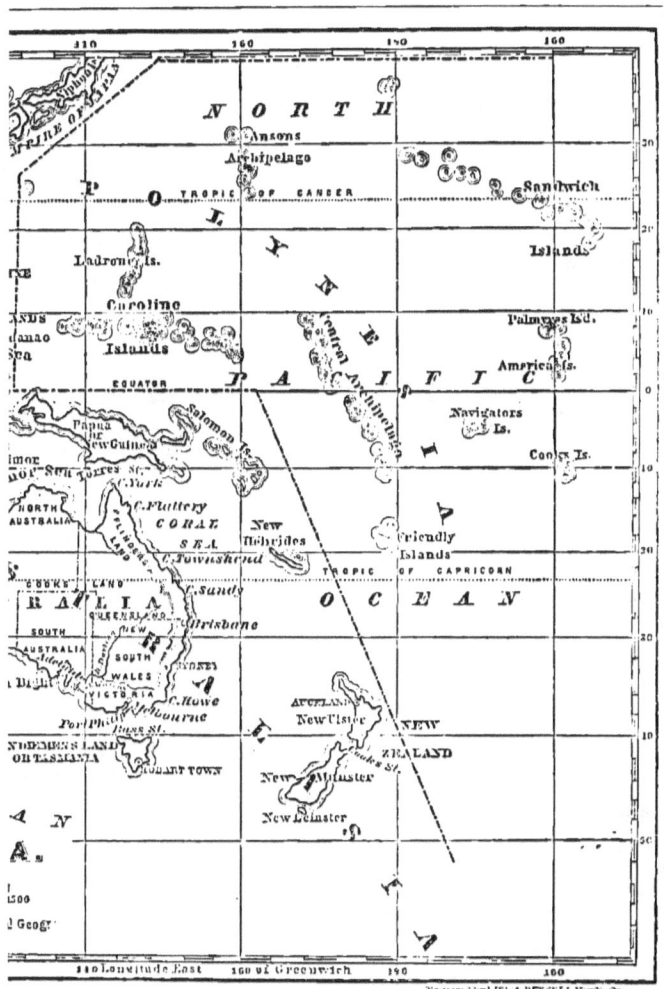

'ortuguese islands.
lo-res, and So-lor.
island in Malaysia.
st and north of Malaysia?

Q. What 8 large islands lie south and east of Malaysia?
Q. Name the British islands in Malaysia.
A. Labuan', and part of Borneo.
Q. Point out the largest island in Australasia.

PRINCIPAL ANIMALS IN OCEANIA.

## EXAMINATION LESSON LXXV.

### Australasia.

*Q.* Point out the position of Australasia.

*Q.* Name the principal islands in this group.

*A.* Australia, Tasmania, New Zealand, New Guinea, New Hebrides, and Salomon Islands.

*Q.* Which of these islands belong to Great Britain?

*A.* Australia, Tasmania, and New Zealand.

## CONVERSATION XLV.

### Conversational Trip through Oceania.

1. From Japan we direct our course southward to the principal islands of Oceania. We first touch at the Philippine islands; and from them proceed onward in succession to the large islands of Borneo, Celebes, Java, &c.

2. From these islands we reach the great island-continent of Australia. Rounding it, we touch at Tasmania, then at New Zealand, and, turning northward, reach the New Hebrides, Salomon Islands, and Papua or New Guinea.

3. From New Guinea we proceed to the Caroline islands, the Ladrones, and the islands in Anson's archipelago. From them we sail eastward of the Sandwich Islands; thence south-west by way of Palmyra's, America's, Cook's, and Navigator's Islands, to the Central Archipelago; and thence south-east and east to the Friendly Islands. We thus make a rapid survey of these great island-clusters in the Pacific Ocean.

*Q.* Trace on the map the trip just made.

*Q.* Point out and name the principal animals of Oceania.

*A.* 1, The Kangaroo-rat; 2, male Kangaroo; 3, female Kangaroo; 4, Duck-billed Platypus; 5, Sheep; 6, Lyre-bird; 7, Cockatoo; 8, Argus-eyed Pheasant; 9, Vulture; 10. Emu; 11, Cassowary; 12, Apteryx, or Wingless-bird; and 13, Black Swan.

## EXAMINATION LESSON LXXVI.

### Australia.

*Q.* Point out the position and boundaries of Australia.

*Q.* Point out and name its capes and gulfs.

*Q.* Into what colonies is it divided?

*A.* Into North, West, and South Australia, Victoria, New South Wales, and Queensland.

AUSTRALIA.

English Miles.

Eng.<sup>l</sup> for Easy Lessons in Gen.<sup>l</sup> Geog.<sup>y</sup>

*Q.* Point out and name its principal mountains.

*A.* The Australian Alps, with several branches, running along the east coast.

*Q.* Point out and name the principal rivers.

*A.* The Darling; with its chief tributaries, —the Lachlan, the Murray, and the Colgoa.

*Q.* What are the chief exports?

*A.* Gold, iron, copper, wool, and tallow.

*Q.* For what is Australia chiefly noted?

*A.* For being the largest island in the world; for its gold; and for its flocks and herds.

*Q.* Point out and name the capital cities.

*A.* Sydney, the capital of New South Wales; Brisbane, of Queensland; Melbourne, of Victoria; Adelaide, of South Australia; and Perth, of West Australia.

---

## CONVERSATION XLVI.

### Conversational Trip among the British Islands of Australasia.

1. Reaching Australia from New Guinea, we first enter the great northern Gulf of Carpentaria, from which we cross North Australia to the west coast. Down this coast we sail until we reach West Australia. Here, rounding Cape Leeuwin, we enter the great Australian Bight, or Gulf, and go up Spencer Gulf into South Australia.

2. Returning by way of Kangaroo Island, we reach Victoria; and turning to the south, across Bass Strait, land at Tasmania, formerly called Van-Diemen's Land, and celebrated as a former penal, or convict, settlement. Crossing this island to Hobart Town, the capital, we sail due east to New Zealand. Here we visit the islands of New Leinster, New Munster, and New Ulster; and embarking at Auckland the capital, return to New South Wales.

3. Touching at Sydney, the capital, we continue our course northward along the coast to Brisbane, the capital of Queensland, and so on to Flinder's Land. Here, taking an inland journey southward, we reach the tributaries of the river Darling. Crossing them and following the Liverpool and the Blue Mountains and the Australian Alps, we arrive at Victoria.

4. Turning westward, we descend the river Murray until we reach the Darling. Crossing this river into South Australia, we visit the great salt-lake Torrens. From it proceeding southward, we come to Spencer Gulf again.

*Q.* Trace on the map (page 75) the trip just made.

## EXAMINATION LESSON LXXVII.

### Tasmania, New Zealand, &c.

*Q.* Point out the position and boundaries of Tasmania.

*Q.* Point out and name the principal capes and straits.

*Q.* Point out the position of New Zealand.

*Q.* Name the principal islands in the group.

*A.* New Ulster, Munster, and Leinster.

*Q.* Point out and name the chief cities.

*A.* Hobart Town, the capital of Tasmania; and Auckland, the capital of New Zealand.

*Q.* Name the principal groups of the Papuan islands.

*A.* New Guinea, Salomon, & New Heb-ri-des.

*Q.* Name the principal island-groups in Polynesia.

*A.* Anson's, Ladrone', Caroline, Sandwich, Navigators', Cook's, Friendly Islands, &c.

*Q.* Which are the most important of these groups?

*A.* The Sandwich Islands, the natives of which have advanced in civilization. Capital, Honolulu.

---

## EXAMINATION LESSON LXXVIII.

### The Continent of Africa.

*Q.* Point out the position and boundaries of Africa.

*Q.* Point out and name its capes, gulfs, and bays.

*Q.* Point out and name its principal rivers.

*A.* The Nile, Lu-fij-i, Zam-be-si, Orange, Con-go, Ni-ger [-jer], and Sen-e-gal [-gaul].

*Q.* Name the principal lakes.

*A.* Tchad, Dem-be-a, Victoria-Ny-an-za, Ta-gan-y-ka, Ny-as-sa, and N'gam-i.

*Q.* Point out and name the principal divisions of Africa.

*A.* The Barbary States, Egypt, Nubia, Abyssinia, Eastern Africa, Southern Africa, Lower and Upper Guinea, Soudan', and the Sa-ha-ra.

*Q.* Point out and name the principal islands.

*A.* Mad-a-gas-car, St. Helena, Ascension, the Cape-Verds, Canaries, & the Ma-dei-ras [-day-].

*Q.* What are the chief exports?

*A.* Cotton, rice, nuts, ebony, and ivory.

*Q.* For what is Africa chiefly noted?

*A.* For its vast extent, its almost unbroken coast-line, and its great river Nile.

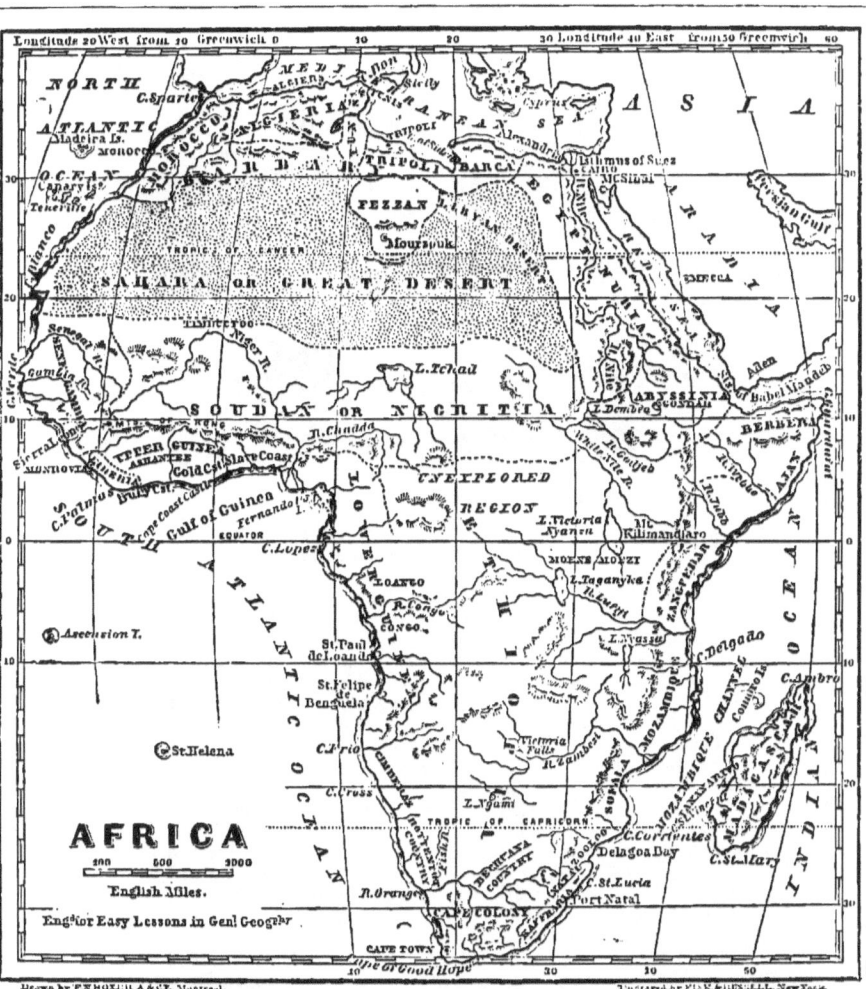

AFRICA

English Miles.

Eng<sup>r</sup> for Easy Lessons in Gen<sup>l</sup> Geog<sup>hy</sup>

Q. What countries lie north of the Sahara Desert?
Q. Point out and name the countries which lie between the Great Desert of Sahara and the Equator.
Q. Point out and name the countries which lie between the ator and the Tropic of Capricorn.

Q. What countries lie south of the Tropic of Capricorn?
Q. Which are the principal rivers at the west of Africa?
Q. Which are the principal rivers at the east of Africa?
Q. What celebrated sea separates Africa from Arabia?
Q. What large island lies off the S.E. coast of Africa?

PRINCIPAL ANIMALS ON THE CONTINENT OF AFRICA.

ION XLVII.

rough the Continent
rica.

ustralia by the Indian
gascar. Crossing this
Mo-zam-bique [-beek]
ast of Africa.
uth, we pass in succes-
he British colonies of
til we reach Cape Col-
Cape of Good Hope,
til past the Hottentot
Lower Guinea.
ea we turn to the west
Coast, Gold Coast, Ash-
-o-ne, and Senegambia,
e to the Senegal river.
st, we reach Barbary.
oast along by Algeria,
ca, until we arrive at

ancient river Nile, we
the capital, and the
our way to Nubia

and Abyssinia. Crossing over to the Strait of
Babelmandeb, we round Cape Guardafui' and
sail southward along the Ajan and Zanguebar'
coast to Mozambique. At Mozambique we
enter the Zambesi river, and follow its course
inland until we reach the great Victoria Falls.
From these falls we turn northward, through
the vast region of Ethiopia, or Central Africa.
Here, in our progress, we meet with tribes
which have never seen the face of a white
man, or heard of the SAVIOUR, but which
still bow down to idols, and worship strange
gods. We find the trees and shrubs and
flowers of luxuriant growth, and of great
beauty. Many of the animals, and of the
birds and reptiles, too, are different from what
we have ever seen or heard of. As we approach
the Great Desert, we cross several tributaries
of the famous Nile (which have not yet been
explored), and extensive lakes and lofty mountains. When we come to this desert, we find
nothing but parched and arid sands, destitute
of trees and water. In order to cross the
desert with safety, travellers are compelled to
join some of the native caravans of camels
which trade between the Barbary States and

the interior, exchanging gold-dust and ivory for the productions of the coast and of foreign countries. At several points on the way the caravans stop at fertile spots in the desert, called oases [o'-à-sees], where water, grass, and trees are found, and where the travellers and camels refresh themselves.

*Q.* Trace on the map the trip just made.

*Q.* Point out, on the opposite page, and name, the principal animals of Africa.

*A.* 1, The Mandril; 2, Baboon; 3, Lion; 4, Hyena; 5, Camel; 6, Cape-Buffalo; 7, Giraffe; 8, Zebra; 9, Elephant; 10, Hippopotamus; 11, Ostrich; 12, Alligator; 13, Cobra-di-Capello, a most venomous serpent.

## EXAMINATION LESSON LXXIX.
### The Four Barbary States.

*Q.* Point out and name the four Barbary States.

*A.* Morocco, Algeria, Tunis; and Tripoli, including its dependencies, Barca and Fezzan'.

*Q.* What range of mountains runs through Morocco and Algeria?

*A.* The Atlas range,—and from it the Atlantic Ocean is named.

*Q.* What islands lie off the Atlantic coast of Morocco?

*A.* The Madeiras, belonging to Portugal.

*Q.* What islands lie south of the Madeira islands?

*A.* The Canaries, belonging to Spain.

*Q.* To whom do the Barbary States belong?

*A.* Algeria belongs to France; but most of the other States are independent.

*Q.* What are the chief exports?

*A.* Olive-oil, fine leather, carpets, wool, indigo.

*Q.* Name and point out the chief cities.

*A.* Morocco, Algiers, Tunis, Tripoli, and Mourzouk'.

## EXAMINATION LESSON LXXX.
### North-Eastern and South-Eastern Africa.

*Q.* Point out the countries of North-Eastern Africa.

*A.* Egypt, Nubia, and Abyssinia.

*Q.* Point out the position and boundaries of each.

*Q.* What river runs through these countries?

*A.* The celebrated river Nile.

*Q.* For what Scripture event is this river noted?

*A.* For the finding of Moses, who had been floated on it, in a little ark of bulrushes.

*Q.* Who placed him in this ark?

*A.* His mother, as King Pharaoh had ordered all the Hebrew infant boys to be thrown into the Nile.

*Q.* By whom was Moses found?

*A.* By the daughter of Pharaoh.

*Q.* What did she do with him?

*A.* She gave him to his mother to be nursed, and brought him up as her own son.

*Q.* What sea lies to the east of Egypt?

*A.* The Red Sea.

*Q.* For what is this sea noted?

*A.* For the passing through it by the Israelites, under Moses, when on their way from Egypt to the promised land of Canaan.

*Q.* What celebrated mount is at the head of this sea?

*A.* Mount Sinai, in Arabia, around which the Israelites encamped.

*Q.* What took place here?

*A.* The Israelites received from GOD, by the hand of Moses, the Ten Commandments.

*Q.* For what is Egypt chiefly noted?

*A.* For its antiquity and its Pyramids.

*Q.* Name and point out its capital cities.

*A.* In Egypt, Cairo; in Abyssinia, Gondar.

*Q.* What are the chief exports?

*A.* Grain, dates, coffee, senna, and ebony.

*Q.* Point out the countries of South-Eastern Africa.

*A.* Berbera, Zanguebar, and Mozambique.

*Q.* Point out the position and boundaries of each.

*Q.* Point out their principal capes.

*Q.* Name and point out their principal rivers.

*A.* The Webbe, Jubb, Lufiji, and Zambesi.

*Q.* What are the chief exports?

*A.* Gold, copper, ivory, and fruits.

## EXAMINATION LESSON LXXXI.
### Central Africa.

*Q.* Point out the chief divisions of Central Africa.

*A.* The Sahara, Soudan, and Ethiopia.

*Q.* Point out the position and boundaries of each.

*Q.* Name and point out the principal lakes.

*A.* Tchad, Victoria-Nyanza, Taganyka, Nyassa, Shirwa, and N'gami.

*Q.* Name and point out the principal rivers.

*A.* The Niger, Lufigi, and Zambezi.

*Q.* In what river are there magnificent falls?

*A.* In the Zambezi are the Victoria Falls.

*Q.* What mountains separate Soudan from Up. Guinea?

*A.* The Kong Mountains, running E. & W.

*Q.* Name and point out the chief city.

*A.* Timbuctoo', on the Niger, in Soudan.

### EXAMINATION LESSON LXXXII.

#### Southern Africa.

*Q.* Name and point out the chief divisions of Southern Africa.

*A.* The Zulu (or Zooloo), Boshuanhas, and Hottentot Countries; and the British coloni of Natal, Kaffraria, and the Cape.

KAFFIR CHIEF OF THE ZULU TRIBE.

*Q.* Point out the position and boundaries of each.

*Q.* Name and point out the principal rivers.

*A.* The Orange and Fish rivers.

*Q.* What are the chief exports?

*A.* Wool, sheep, ivory, and ostrich-feathers.

*Q.* Name and point out the principal cities.

*A.* Cape Town and Port Natal.

### EXAMINATION LESSON LXXXIII.

#### Lower and Upper Guinea, &c.

*Q.* Name and point out the chief divisions of Lower Guinea.

*A.* Congo and Loango.

*Q.* Name and point out the chief divisions of Upper Guinea.

*A.* Slave Coast, Gold Coast, Ashantee; and Liberia, a republic of freed American slaves.

*Q.* How are these countries governed?

*A.* The Gold-Coast Settlements by the British and the Dutch: the others are independent.

*Q.* Point out the position and boundaries of each.

*Q.* What are the chief exports?

*A.* Gold-dust, palm-oil, ivory, and maize.

*Q.* Name and point out the chief city.

*A.* Cape-Coast Castle (British).

*Q.* Name and point out the chief town in Liberia.

*A.* Monrovia, the capital.

*Q.* Name and point out the chief divisions of Senegambia and adjoining countries.

*A.* Senegal, Gambia, and Sierra Le-o-ne.

*Q.* What are the chief exports?

*A.* Timber, hides, cotton, and palm-oil.

*Q.* How are these countries governed?

*A.* The French have settlements on the Senegal river. The British have settlements on the Gambia river: they have also Sierra Leone, a colony for freed African slaves.

*Q.* Name and point out the principal rivers.

*A.* The Senegal and the Gambia.

### EXAMINATION LESSON LXXXIV.

#### The Islands of Africa.

*Q.* Name and point out the principal islands of Africa.

*A.* Madagascar, St. Helena, Ascension, Fernando Po', the Canaries, and the Madeiras.

*Q.* Name and point out the British islands.

*A.* Mauritius, the Sey-chelles', St. Helena, Ascension, and a northern part of Madagascar.

*Q.* Name and point out the French islands.

*A.* Bourbon, Ste. Marie, Nossibé, Mayotta.

*Q.* Name and point out the principal Spanish islands.

*A.* The Canaries and Fernando Po.

*Q.* Name and point out the Portuguese islands.

*A.* The Madeiras, the Azores, and the Cape-Verds (the last lying off Cape Verde).

*Q.* Is Madagascar independent? Name its capital.

*A.* It is chiefly independent. Tananarivo, in the centre, is its capital.

THE END.